MICROSCOPY

MICROSCOPY

REMI ALBERT

ARCHWAY
PUBLISHING

Archway Publishing books may be ordered through booksellers or by contacting:

Archway Publishing
1663 Liberty Drive
Bloomington, IN 47403
www.archwaypublishing.com
1 (888) 242-5904

ISBN: 978-1-4808-1544-5 (sc)
ISBN: 978-1-4808-1545-2 (e)

Library of Congress Control Number: 2015902035

Print information available on the last page.

Archway Publishing rev. date: 3/13/2015

CONTENTS

CHAPTER 1

MASSACRE AT "THE AVENUE"

Many broken men have gazed upon this ominous skyline and longed for absolution.

A slight morning rain dulls the busy streets of a grand metropolis. The solemn scene provides a feeling of slow motion that perpetuate the doldrums while prompting the stale smell of saturated streets, worn rubber, and noxious emissions that contaminate the already thick atmosphere. Taxicabs and larger forms of saleable transportation share the crowded roads with commuters and their infinite variety of automobiles. Denying conformity, they share a strong tenacity to reflect their individualism.

However, traffic borders a black wave of umbrellas rolling down the sidewalks as pedestrians block the rain on their arbitrary journeys, comically resembling worker ants returning to their hills and entering the vast maze of tunnels underneath. Or in this case, above.

The seemingly scripted society arranges everyone in their part quite accurately. Marching in cadence, the suits enter large skyscrapers and ascend to a world of cubicles, fax machines, and progress reports, while the uniforms either stride into their accepted prowess or hop out of their corresponding business vehicles and enter a world of total commercial access. Occasional vendors, street performers, and the destitute maintain their lifestyle moment by moment trying desperately to persevere through widespread economic uncertainty.

Tucked in among the chaos that is infrastructure and greatly overshadowed by its towering neighbors, a small diner happens to claim one corner. A long, dark-green, wooden sign, bearing gold trim and engraved gold lettering that reads, "The Avenue," hangs above the doorway.

Patrons and new comers shuffle in and out of the entrance frequently, eating on the go being the status quo of the concrete jungle.

Considering the simple yet elegant appearance outside, the diner is fairly spacious and homey inside. Through the doorway, the counter-slash-bar sits back against the wall while the dining floor opens to the right. Seating to accommodate maybe fifty people is occupied by business consultants, stockbrokers, investors, and even the lonely receptionists.

The diner's staff consists of half-a-dozen teenage girls, all skinny with long, dark hair, and an insatiable ability to charm blossoming entrepreneurs. Three young males either work the busing details or assist the servers by rolling out large bread couriers that offer customers fresh bagels, rolls, or English muffins.

A husband and wife partnership diligently works the counter taking payments or fulfilling the needs of the barstool patrons.

Samuel and Rosie Vincent took over ownership of The Avenue after Samuel's uncle left him the restaurant. This inheritance came from a nasty dispute concerning the last will and testament resulting in his uncle's own daughter being conveniently skipped.

Rosie is a broad shouldered woman with a loud voice and a strong enough presence to gain the respect of even the social elite. Her husband is tall and round but lacks the same towering approach. He frantically scurries about emitting both a sense of duty and intimidation, as if he were a soldier behind enemy lines with a clear focus on his objective. The day persists just the same way it always does: fast forward.

Among today's guests, six black suits sit around the large conference table in the center of the dining area conversing at random. At the head of the table sits Eugene Broussard, an intimidating figure resembling more of a lumberjack than a businessman. His father owned a chain of successful pharmacies that Eugene liquidated once he inherited a majority of the shares. The proceeds were later invested into a medical research laboratory that now boasts the largest shareholdings in the prescription drug market, Eugene being the active chief executive.

To Broussard's immediate right sits Tyler Graham Vaughn, no more a medical researcher than Eugene is a logrolling champion. A stockbroker redundantly turned investor, Tyler moved up the ranks by the usual means: buy low, sell high. Little more than a checkbook, Tyler's knowledge of market trends enables stability in the company's budget.

Further on down the table, Dr. Charles Mendel sits to Vaughn's right. Mendel is one of only two actual doctors on the executive board. Starting his career as a developer, Mendel's work is partly the reason people can now combat acid reflux disease. It was his breakthroughs that spawned an era of development in which suppressants became the financial foundation for all medical facilities.

Adjacent to Mendel, to Broussard's left, sits Miles Johnston. A long-time partner to Broussard, Miles systematically breaks down competitive industries, collecting shares that hemorrhage value due to inconsistencies during off-peak seasons. Tyler Vaughn acts as Miles's understudy offering tips on which companies to pursue. They weave awfully twisted webs.

Besides Miles sits Dr. Mumahd Zehata, the second of the two doctors who reside on the board. Mumahd's father, Satieri, came to the States in the seventies as an ear, nose, and throat specialist. A successful partnership with an unknown inventor gave way for the development of endoscopy. Satieri helped pave the way for Mumahd to disband his medical practice and begin investing in the research and development aspect.

And last but not least, at the foot of the table rests Karen Vicelli. In her late twenties, the young exec is the only daughter of the late CEO, Tony Vicelli. Karen graduated valedictorian as an accounting major through the school of business from a well-known Ivy League school. Her responsibilities include basic bookkeeping, checks and balances/gains and losses, taxation, and so on and so forth.

Karen acts as cousin to Samuel Vincent, who was actually born Seneaco Vicelli. Karen is the uncle's daughter who was skipped over for the inheritance of The Avenue.

With all the major players in place, the chess match is about to begin.

The conference table is all a buzz this day at The Avenue. Board members, representing the brain trust of the deceased founder, Tony Vicelli, talk of adding a new developer to their plethora.

Tony created Magnus Medical Distribution Corporation by purchasing and consolidating independent research facilities as a way to merely gain breaks from competing insurance giants while consequently increasing one's profit value. Now with over forty-three percent of the global market, as far as Magnus's competition is concerned, check mate.

The board members discuss their distribution of Neurolex, an old compound proposed by Dr. Mendel that originated back at his own developmental laboratory over five years ago. Now the subsequent developer pitches an upgraded version for their consideration. The discussions are so heated that many of the standpoints cannot be deciphered out of the insistent bantering, nor can their attention be redirected toward the lone mysterious figure that just entered the diner.

This unknown figure wears a solid-blue hooded sweatshirt that's been pulled up over his head. The man makes no eye contact. He maintains his focus downward as if trying to avoid cracks in the floor out of some superstition. Not even fifteen feet into the restaurant, the figure slows his walk, gaining the attention of both Samuel and Rosie along with a few employees and restaurant patrons. A moment of silence freezes time as the figure comes to a halt. All the while, his hands are tucked within the hoodie's front pouch.

Before Samuel can even mutter, "May I help you?" the hooded figure pulls a nine-millimeter handgun from its cozy hiding spot while simultaneously turning toward the conference table and taking aim at Magnus's executive board of sitting ducks.

The figure finally breaks his silence with a word, "One." The gun's fiery discharge illuminates the frightened faces of the diners. It precedes a bloodcurdling scream that Karen bellows, shedding light on the first bullet's trajectory. Karen stands up quickly, staring at the red dot on Eugene's button-down. As the bloodstain slowly spreads, Eugene Broussard's state of shock diminishes and he sinks back into his chair and falls to the floor.

The restaurant erupts with screams. People scramble from their chairs in search of cover.

"Two." The second shot enters Tyler Graham Vaughn's side. As he is spinning in retreat, the bullet enters high on the ribs, passing through his chest cavity, and exiting via the armpit. The projectile continues on, striking down a fleeing patron. While Vaughn's body falls sideways and bounces off of the nearby table, the shattering of plates and glassware as they all come crashing to the ground isn't loud enough to cover the word, "Three."

Dr. Charles Mendel takes a shot in the back but doesn't fall forward. He spins wildly to the right, colliding with Karen Vicelli en route to her own hiding place. As they fall, Mendel's lifeless body falls onto Karen's legs and pins her down.

"Four." The fourth shot finds Johnston. Miles Johnston thinks meticulously, figuring that the kitchen area is safe behind closed push-doors. While making a run for it, the bullet enters his back as well. Miles falls forward into the swinging doors and his body ends up lining the tile floor halfway between the kitchen and the dining area with the swinging doors propped open at his sides.

"Five." Zehata shares his round. Dr. Mumahd Zehata suffers the worst wound by taking the bullet in the neck. Born of an ear, nose, and throat specialist, Zehata took pride in his perfect septum. However, ironically, it's now deviated. The bullet not only tears the spine but also opens a blood wound in the trachea, above the lungs, to where Mumahd does not die from the gunshot but from drowning in his own blood. Lying on the floor and grasping his throat, Mumahd spits and gurgles for air.

"Six." Karen Vicelli tries frantically to free herself by methodically pushing on Mendel's body to gain momentum, trying to roll him off with strength and inertia. Pulling her legs out ever so slightly as she rolls, Karen doesn't sustain the presence of mind to notice her surroundings. The mysterious figure is well aware of his immobilized prey. He simply walks up to the last remaining member of the Vicelli trademark and fires. The final target is executed by a direct hit to the center of her forehead.

"Seven." The mysterious figure has one final objective after all. He places the gun underneath his jaw and tilts his head back. He then closes his eyes and pulls the trigger. The bullet lodges in the ceiling while the figure in the blue hooded sweatshirt falls quietly to the floor, ending the massacre.

No one knew who he was. Nobody knew what he wanted. But now the entire executive board of the Magnus Medical Distribution Corporation lies motionless on the floor, leaving one large gap of uncertainty within the company's future. One thing is known, The Avenue will never be the same.

CHAPTER 2

MICROSCOPIC ASSASSINS

Overhead lighting casts its vivid glow upon seven covered bodies arranged on stainless steel examination tables. A lone physician, wearing his long, white coat, blends almost seamlessly with the light-colored walls of the Medical Examiner's autopsy room. He begins his procedure on the body of the unknown assailant in the blue hooded sweatshirt.

Outside from the media spectacle growing around the entrance of St. John's Medical Center, and the armed guards stationed by the autopsy room doors, the physician is at total peace to perform his duties. He slowly prods around the unknown figure's wound, starting from under the jaw and extending through the top of his skull. Strangely, a small circle of red ink has been drawn on his throat around the entry wound. It must've happened at the scene. The unknown figure's face is finally revealed to be that of an old man's, not the young, skinny, possible drug addict that his appearance suggested.

The physician, thirty-two year old Bradley Simpson, takes careful time not to rush his protocol, though mounting questions and concerns surrounding this massacre dramatically inflate the pressure.

Bradley, short dark hair and well groomed, was born from a very strict family where the expectation to succeed was more of a legacy than a value. His uncompromising work has led to the conviction of countless perpetrators whose subtle methods prove too much for basic forensics. A man of great detail, Bradley Simpson now realizes that *he's* the one on the liable chopping block.

Bradley approaches the exit wound to search the flared opening of hair, blood, and bone for evidence of bullet fragmentation. He observes a tiny black spec floating in the clear, bloodstained cerebrospinal fluid discharging from the brain cavity. As steady as a gymnast, Bradley clenches a pair of surgical tweezers and moves in for the extraction.

Just when he's about to grab the foreign fragment, a small electrical arc shoots out from the spec and into the tips of his tweezers. Surprised but not injured, Bradley pulls back and in the usual fashion under such circumstances exclaims, "What the hell was that?"

Bradley goes back in after the fragment, and again, a little electrical arc meets his tweezers. This time however, he succeeds in grasping the tiny spec and removing it from the unknown figure's skull.

Bradley turns and nonchalantly makes his way over to his trusty microscope. Grabbing a nearby Petri dish on his way, the renowned physician places his catch down as he's done countless times, slides the trey under the telescopic lens, and leans in for further examination.

Dr. Simpson, for the first time in his illustrious career, is shocked at what he sees. He has no idea.

The tiny spec appears to be thousands of microscopic robots mechanically programmed to clump together for some form or function. The robots resemble insects. Red light emitting diodes constitute visual acuity at the forefront of their black arachnid body mass while a set of jagged pincers are protruding from what would be the mandible of any arthropod. Beyond astonished, Bradley reaches for the clump with his tweezers again, and again the clump

fires an electric shock. But this time he witnesses the source of
the energy. Electricity is forced from the body mass of each bug to
generate power through the legs and eventually to the whole pod
until encompassing the entire structure. Tiny fibers on the hooked
extremities, along with the pincers, allow these robotic bugs to latch
upon one another with an almost inseparable force.

Bradley decides to try and separate the pod as to further dissect
his new find. He grabs another pair of tweezers and moves in, bridges
the circuit once more, and grasps a hold of the pod from either side.
Small static sparks jump from the pod and into the tips of his tweezers, shocking the doctor's fingers as he works. Pulling with all his
might, Bradley struggles to break the robot's grip, but they begin
to gradually loosen and pull apart. The sudden separation triggers
a power surge that not only charges Dr. Simpson with nearly one
hundred and ten volts, but it also terminates the pod in the process.
Bradley jumps back in pain from the shock and drops the tweezers,
like he might if he'd just shoved them into the wall socket.

Meanwhile, an unknown presence pushes the door open and
makes its way into the autopsy room. Unaware, Bradley recollects
his tweezers and returns to his microscope. As he leans back in to
look at the charred pod, he notices movement out of the corner of
his eye. But unlike the way the suave James Bond types react, the
doctor surprisingly jumps back and sort of gasps in a high-pitched
voice, consequently scaring the shit out of Detective Dunbar as well.

Paige Dunbar, the presence, is a lifelong resident of the big city.
She's a fourth-generation cop that was promoted to detective after
uncovering an underground gambling ring of stocks, bonds, and
corporate bank notes, indicting many well-known public officials
as well as four fellow officers.

The detective jumps backwards when Dr. Simpson surprises
her and she draws her sidearm just in case he meant not to be
discovered.

Dr. Simpson aptly raises his hands and declares, "Whoa, shit! Don't shoot!"

"What in the hell is wrong with you?" demands Detective Dunbar as she attempts to calm her nerves while also putting her gun away.

"I'm sorry, I didn't see you standing there," answers Bradley, concluding such an awkward introduction.

While putting his hands down, Dr. Simpson scans over Detective Dunbar. She is fairly attractive for an authority figure. Her long, straight, black hair shines enough to accent the lacquered finish on her utility belt and the polished steel of her issue. Her face is small and easy to look at, with no weird scars or signs of brutal entanglements from battling with the underbelly of society. And her body is slim and petite but with a definite tone. She's not diesel with broad shoulders and bulging lady-muscles. In short, she's kind of cute.

"Who are you?" pleads the brave doctor.

"Detective Paige Dunbar," replies the mysterious presence. "I'm looking for Dr. Brady Simpson."

"It's Bradley actually. What can I do for you, Detective?" Bradley withdraws back to his microscope and specimen with a coy innocence while Detective Dunbar makes her way through the room to observe the bodies.

"They're ready for your report," the detective declares while staying focused on the cadavers.

"They're, who?" The good doctor isn't well aware of the gravity of his discovery and the victims chosen.

"The police. The media. They want answers." Detective Dunbar arbitrarily scans over the victims as if trying to pinpoint the cause of death.

The doctor evades her questionnaire, "They got shot. What more do you need to know?"

The detective looks up at Bradley and persists, "Why them?"

Bradley buries his face into the microscope hoping that maybe his distractive deportment would defuse the detective's curiosity. "I suspect the same reason why any desperate man shoots successful people, envy." The PhD evades well.

"But six executive board members, all at the same place, all at the same time?" Detective Dunbar follows her protocol well.

"Coincidence." Dr. Simpson with the comeback.

Paige finally continues, "Well, what have you got so far?"

"Not much, I've only worked on the shooter," Bradley doesn't lie. "Short of a few fragments, it was a clean exit. Toxicology will take a couple of days."

Detective Dunbar can't help but notice that Bradley hasn't removed his attention from the sample under any circumstances. Curiously she implies, "What have you got there?"

Dr. Simpson is pretty sure that the detective didn't hear his heart sink, but the question still sent a chill down his spine. Nervously, but without hesitation, Bradley looks up and replies, "One of the fragments I extracted from the shooter's skull. Shall I show you his cranial fracture?" Bradley then returns to his microscope.

Somberly recluse, the detective gathers her boundaries and concludes, "I'll leave you to your work then, Doctor. Thank you for your time." Detective Paige Dunbar exits the room with a slow-paced remorsefulness.

Bradley looks up with a stunned reprieve as the detective leaves. The conspiracy at hand can only be met with discretion unless he's willing to accept retaliation for uncovering the truth. Dr. Bradley Simpson chooses to continue working. He makes his way over to the examination tables with a decision in mind.

The high-pitched squeal of an electrical tool rises to its deafening peak. Dr. Simpson takes the hand-held, angled arm circular saw and starts his incision along the hairline of the mysterious figure in the blue hood. After encompassing the skull, Bradley sets his tool down and grasps the hair firmly. Placing his foot on the leg of the examination table for leverage, and with one swift tug, Dr. Bradley Simpson opens up a can of worms.

A few hours later...

Four, tiny, blood-soaked specs lie harmlessly on a white towel that rests in a stainless steel trey beside the operating tables. Bradley continues his autopsy on the rest of the shooter's body. Diagnosis thus far includes the cerebellum, the cerebral cortex or central fissure, the medulla oblongata, the hypothalamus or pituitary gland, and the first specimen, which leaked out of the cerebrum, unknown. Each pod is specifically networked to interrupt higher brain functions so that they can control the carrier signals throughout the mind and body.

The cerebellum controls your coordination and the body's ability to maintain equilibrium. The central fissure offers bodily sensation. The medulla controls anything from breathing to blood flow. And the pituitary gland maintains temperature, hunger, and thirst.

Signalized pulses are sent from these pods throughout the nerves to trick the brain into thinking the body is either deprived of something or in excess. The bugs can introduce an objective that weighs on the mind of the recipient until the objective is carried out. So in essence, the shooter was more of a remote-controlled zombie than a man. As Bradley removed each pod from his body, the sudden breakage from the tissue fibers and/or proximity to the brain waves, destroyed the mechanism and also fried the host's nerve receptors, causing what would've been permanent damage to any live person. They're not so harmless after all.

Toxicology Report: Negative. Except it appears the shooter had been drinking heavily leading up to the spree. Blood Alcohol Content: Seventeen percent. He knew that he'd been programmed or activated, but tried to refuse the urge, drown his distortions. Most disturbing.

Dr. Simpson wraps up his work on the first body. The once aggressor is now a possible victim.

CHAPTER 3

N.E.T.I. PHARMACEUTICALS

Streets in the big city are chaotic at worst. Given the overabundant amount of people that bypass the city's heart on a daily basis, they coexist quite efficiently. Not even the yellow caution tape and newly boarded windows of The Avenue can hinder the spirit of such a high demanding, moneymaking corollary.

Not far beyond the sky-rises and overlooking the city, a small, secure facility is located within the foothills of the surrounding terrain. Sort of resembling a veterinarian hospital from the look, the one-story facility seems placed inconspicuously, other than the electrified barbed wire fence that guards its property.

The fence's main gate slowly retracts to allow three black SUV's to pass. The vehicles don't have to answer a call box or press a code into a security pad, a presence upholds the gate at all times. The tint over the truck's windows sheds no light on the occupants, but the arrangement of stars on the license plate indicates military. The anonymous visitors pull around to the back of the building while the gate rolls closed along an electric powered guide track. A back-up generator for the gate exists in the guard station.

Once inside, the facility looks as expected: light-colored walls, sterile everything, freezing cold, blinding lighting, etc. However, this institution does not allow the full access that a public hospital might. Each research station is visible through windows while electronically sealed doors provide the only entrance to each room. The working physicians must all wear decontamination suits as well as pass through a sanitization system before entering the clean rooms. (Goggles, gloves, shoe sleeves, the works. No exceptions.)

Short of the main laboratory's entrance, the occupants from the unmarked utility vehicles make their way down the central corridor toward the decon room. The visitors all wear military dress that's been spackled with ribbons, awards, and stars (both silver and gold). They're obviously the highest-ranking officials in their respective branches.

Led by an apparent physician, they enter the spray chamber and basically are deloused before suited for admittance. Piloted by a fellow physician, the first tour of N.E.T.I. Pharmaceuticals is about to commence, N.E.T.I. being short for Neurological Engineering Technology Institute. Widely accredited in the medical underground for its successful computer mapping of the entire human body, N.E.T.I. developed methods of administering medication that can be networked to specific areas or ailments whereas concentrating the dose, or as the medical world calls it, immunized localization.

The authority figures, led by their guides, enter the main laboratory. Already waiting inside and dressed in his static-free ensemble, the subsequent doctor of Dr. Charles Mendel, Dr. Walter Truax stands alert mimicking an unrenowned scientist on his first day of demonstration.

"Welcome, gentlemen. I'm glad all of you could make it." Walter opens with a mechanically distorted tone for his greeting. Being that general dust masks are not suitable for this environment, specialized breathing apparatuses must be worn to minimize infectivity. Audio transmitters in the masks allow for communication. Walter continues.

"This facility, as you know, demonstrates the cutting edge of medical research. Contributing breakthroughs in scientific technology that render conventional medicine practically useless. You're all standing in what is the developmental stage of our nano-robotics technology."

The military tourists watch as the lab workers manufacture what appears to be absolutely nothing. The Petri dishes seem to be filled with some strange type of black sand. The black grains ripple, wave, and roll up and down almost like water. Outfitted with everything from electron microscopes to magnified goggles, the workers primarily peer through small screens while operating a joystick that controls a tiny robotic arm. The arm works sporadically, lifting and stabbing down on the Petri dish as if systematically placing computer chips or transistors into a motherboard. The workers never break their concentration.

"What are they doing?" Lieutenant Colonel Sheppard curiously ponders. Lt. Col. Mark Sheppard has worked beside unmanned drones for over twelve years now, beginning his experience on lethal ground roving vehicles. The concept of microscopic bugs for the sake of reconnaissance and intelligence came to the Lt. Colonel's attention a couple of years ago after an offensive in Kabul failed due to a miscalculation in the enemy's numbers and assets.

Dr. Truax proudly answers, "They are programming the specimens for application."

"What specimens?" Lt. Col. Sheppard asks.

"Precisely." Dr. Truax replies. "A new generation of microscopic engineering is being developed right before your eyes. Technology of such magnitude, that you'd have no way to defend against it or even see it coming."

Walter guides his visitors over to one of the programming stations. A computer monitor displays an image from the electron microscope in which the worker manages the encoding. A series of shocks to the Petri dish liven thousands of robotic bugs. The military personnel jump back with the creeps as they observe these tiny machines crawling over each other with an abiding ambition to find their host.

"Any connection or electrical presence excites the bugs. They strive on establishing their own integration to whatever host we program it to affix." Dr. Truax surprises the group.

"So you're saying that you can bug the human body in the same way you can bug a telephone?" A strained General Taylor questions. General Robert Taylor has served in the United States Army for just over twenty-three years now. He was first deployed to Bosnia in the early nineties, and after multiple tours in Kuwait, Kosovo, Iraq, and Saudi Arabia, General Taylor spends a majority of his time working counter intelligence to help strategize ground troop formations in an ever-growing style of urban warfare. His invite to this demonstration came in part, to his sense of duty and constant ambition to gain any scientific or technological advantage on the battlefield.

"Exactly," Dr. Truax answers the General while continuing to captivate, "Please observe."

The lab worker sends a higher-voltage shock to the Petri dish and wildly excites the bugs. They bump and bang into each other, crawling over anything in their way until they reach a certain group of robots where they begin to attach together and construct a sphere. Within seconds, five, small, individual pods form in the dish. Perfectly rounded, the pea-sized pods carry a constant electrical field that encompasses their mass.

Dr. Walter Truax carefully reaches down with a pair of tweezers and plucks one of the pods from the dish before turning back to his guests.

"Gentlemen, this single pod contains over ten thousand individual bugs all programmed to seek out and attach itself to...Dr. Hileman?"

Dr. Truax turns to his middle-aged lab worker for his answer and she self-effacingly replies, "The superior vena cava, Doctor."

"Thank you." Walter complies.

The particular vein, one of two large veins leading to the right atrium, carries blood from the head and arms to the heart, serving as an ideal interception point for a robotic pod to manage the diastole phase and control blood flow by electronically collapsing the valves that lead to the ventricles. (Awfully complicated shit.)

"The superior vena cava is a vein in the heart that allows us to disrupt blood flow by intermittently shocking the valves to deny proper function, in essence, stopping the heart." Walter succeeds in stunning the crowd yet again. A moment of silence ensues before an upsurge of questions and comments follow.

"You can't do that!" "Are you out of your mind?" "You won't get away with it." "You're a mad man!" - To name a few.

Dr. Walter Truax isn't exactly pleased with his panel's response, so he is compelled to make an executive decision. He starts his approach with cunning appeal.

"Gentlemen, relax. This technology was not developed to control the body. I was merely saying that, given the nature of the ailment and the need for operating, we can utilize these pods to perform countless procedures."

General Dobbs strikes back. "Will they be flushed from the body after the procedure is completed?" General William R. Dobbs is a thirty-year service man. A proud member of the Marine Corps, General Dobbs has been on more ground, in more countries, and has seen more blood spilled on the fronts then most men care to remember. His presence today is in strict regard for the care, safety, and preservation of his troops in the field and any advancement made available.

"That is one of their fail-safes." Walter replies knowing he's running out of time. He cautiously speeds up his decision. Dr. Truax turns to the specimens and carefully grabs the whole dish before he slowly turns back to his audience and proclaims, "Each pod is specifically designed for a particular area of the body as its target. Only through ingestion can these robots then enter the stomach. The acid dissolves their capsule and breaks them apart, they disperse, and then individually rendezvous to the pre-programmed destination where they're realigned and attached to the host. We coat the bugs to match any pill form pending on the size of the affliction. The more pills consumed, the greater their effectiveness."

All the while, Walter has cunningly placed each of the five pods in the palms of two Generals, Dobbs and Taylor, one Lt. Col. Sheppard, one full Colonel Weaver, and one Captain Garrett. Dr. Truax's explanation was enough of a diversion to gain the trust of those ungrateful critics that spoke out against his invention earlier. He softly grabs each pod with his tweezers then gently sets them down into the gloves of the intended.

As Walter's monologue of the robot's basic function, rate of success, and market value comes to an end, the pods appear to gradually shrink in the palms of their victims. And as before, there's a sudden upsurge of questions and comments.

"What is this?" "What's going on here?" "What's happening?" "What have you done to us?" - Dr. Truax has lied.

In fact, the pods didn't need to be ingested after all. As soon as they came in contact with the static electricity residing in each military official's body, the robots activated. Though the static-free suits were thought to protect them from infection, they forgot their faces were only covered with goggles and respirators, leaving many seams, openings, and kinks in their armor. The pods appear to shrink because as each microscopic robot detaches from the pod, it disappears and curiously crawls up the arm of its new proprietor. They're small enough to crawl into the very pores of our skin and eventually into our bloodstream where they constantly circumnavigate the entire structure until reuniting with each other and forming the pod. By now, even Dr. Truax and his assistants can assume to be infected.

The five officials brush their arms and chests wildly in hopes of fighting off their attackers, but even the tens or hundreds they may knock off, thousands remain. After dancing and jumping around for a minute or two, the authority figures finally gather themselves. They look over their suits one last time for something they can't see anyways, and then adjust back to their commanding reserve.

General Dobbs ponders, "We're not dead?"

Walter chuckles before assuring him, "Nor should you be."

"I don't get it, weren't they suppose to stop our hearts?" Lt. Col. Sheppard remarks disappointed.

"It takes them hours to travel to their destination and days, even sometimes weeks, to reassemble back into the pod. But trust when I say, gentlemen, your days are numbered." Dr. Truax drops the bomb.

"You're a monster." Lt. Col. Sheppard claims.

"You won't get away with this." General Dobbs intimidates.

Dr. Traux finally decides to enlighten his visitors on his true intentions. "Gentlemen, we are in the middle of a most opportune time. As you know, Magnus Distribution Corporation was suddenly blindsided by the murder of its entire executive board, leaving its stock options blowing in the wind. Investors are backing out left and right at an astonishing rate. What you don't know, is that Magnus is comprised of five main distributors whose shares are now selling at an all time low. And they're all in need of proper supervision."

General Taylor catches on quickly. "So you want each of us to take up management of these pharmaceutical companies?"

"With my connections in the FDA, we'll control over forty percent of the prescription drug market. A portion of the proceeds will go to the FDA to ensure placement approval, and then ten percent a piece to the insurance companies involved, amounting to billions in revenue. We'll become ridiculously wealthy men."

"There's no way these companies will allow us to take over." Colonel Weaver confidently responds. Colonel Donald Weaver has twenty-eight years in the Air Force under his belt. He first got his wings training a majority of his flight hours in F-14 Tomcats, but later upgrades to the F-18 Hornet and F-22 Raptor provided a much needed computer integration for more manageable flight control and maneuverability. Colonel Weaver now oversees the programming and flight execution of UAD's, unmanned aerial drones. His invite came as an opportunity to leave the large, bulky, aerial drones behind and turn his exacting and calculating demeanor over to a microscopic version.

However, Walter has done his homework in regards of this business venture. "These companies are all government and private funded. It's simple. The more the private funding pulls out, the more the government controls the majority. People need their prescriptions. They will need us to take over and they'll welcome it with open arms, and wallets."

"You *are* mad." Lt. Col. Sheppard is convinced.

"That, or you can all die here and now. It makes no difference to me." Dr. Walter Truax is not the man to trifle with.

"What did you say?" General Taylor sounds generally concerned.

"How dare you." While General Dobbs just sounds pissed.

Truax continues, "I wish it wouldn't have come to this point. Allow me to demonstrate. Doctor?"

Walter turns to his lab worker and she presses the enter key on her computer. A magnetic pulse suddenly flashes from the ceiling and fills the room with a blue, incandescent light. The military officials all take cover but to no avail. Members of the demonstration start dropping like flies. Only those that were handed a pod earlier, and a few others, survive the pulse. As the blue light fades away and the survivors begin to stand, Walter makes a sadistic remark, "It's amazing. The turnover rate at most medical facilities anymore." Everyone else surveys the lab room in horror as the bodies of cameramen, media, military, and even susceptible physicians lay dead on the floor.

Dr. Walter Truax is in fact, not a monster. He's the devil himself.

CHAPTER 4

UNWELCOME VISITORS

Small crowds of media gather near St. John's Medical Center waiting for an update on the victims from the massacre.

A young news anchor stands outside the hospital in front of the Medical Examiner's entrance poised to offer her morning report. "This is Abra Malone reporting for Live Action News on the city's south side. Wednesday's massacre, which resulted in the death of ten people, including six executive board members of the Magnus Medical Distribution Corporation, has finally unveiled an autopsy report shedding light on the city's worst crime in over fifty years. At approximately nine-thirty a.m. Wednesday morning, a figure wearing a blue hooded sweatshirt, whose name is being withheld from the public, entered The Avenue restaurant downtown and opened fire. Witnesses reported the gunman specifically targeting the board members, acting out more of an assassination plot than a crime of passion. Seven of the ten victims were taken here to St. John's Medical Center where Medical Examiner, Dr. Bradley Simpson, performed the autopsies. The other three victims were taken directly to the County Coroner's Office where no report has been made on either their identity or any autopsy results. Though not available for comment himself, Dr. Simpson's report concluded that all six members of Magnus died from the results of their wounds, while the shooter apparently had a blood alcohol content of point-two-eight, which is over triple the legal limit. Authorities are further investigating ties that the assailant might've had with the executive board or the corporation itself. In the meantime, the prescription drug giant's stock values have continued to plummet at nearly ten percent daily, clouding the future of the Magnus Corporation trademark. We're going to continue following this story as it develops. Reporting live outside St. John's Medical Center, this is Abra Malone."

Though he wasn't lying about the results from the victim's autopsies, it appears our hero Dr. Simpson, took the discretionary approach in regards of the shooter.

When not at work, Bradley assumes the role of loving husband and caring father. He sits comfortably at home watching the afternoon news. Miss Malone's report grasped his attention, but only for the sake of reassurance that his secret wasn't revealed.

Bradley lives in a very modest home. No over dramatic profligacy, no gaudy materialistic fixation, no impressionistic bullshit. Respectably practical.

Bradley's wife, Audrey Simpson, sits at her study typing out a thesis for her eager apprentices. Born Audrey Hilliard, she dedicated her life to human rights. And not just the idea, the actual application. Audrey is the daughter of a psychiatrist and a financial advisor, uniting into one smart cookie with the ability of sociological profiling. Founder of her own online organization, Audrey gathers private lenders to back work-related insurance lawsuits, not only compensating the injured, but enforcing the modernization of safety precautions and equipment while ensuring a cut on the lender's end. That is if they win the case.

Possessing this "power of the people" quality, she's referred to as a cyber-attorney, hence the future apprentices, with a heart like Robin Hood's. In which case, she's neither.

Bradley and Audrey met in graduate school during a protest

against stem-cell research and the fetuses required for theory test. Audrey's passion for justice inevitably shadows her personality which mocks a blend of Lucille Ball hiding the determination of General Patton.

- A silly hard-ass, go figure.

Audrey excels at shooter games on the Xbox that she shares with her eight year old son Jacob. Their battles are awfully fierce, but Audrey usually wins. Jacob wins every so often. He's getting better.

Bradley on the other hand, sucks something awful at videogames. He can manage tweezers, tools, and thousands of dollars in equipment with absolute stillness, but give him a joystick and four multi-colored buttons and the mechanical skills go right out the window.

- Again, go figure.

However, Jacob isn't playing his videogames today. His friends stopped by the house earlier riding their bikes and heading in the direction of freedom and adventure filled with cuts, bruises, and the occasional popped chain that immobilizes the pedals pull on the gears. Jacob tolerated a moment of ridicule as his mom insisted that if he wanted to go out riding, he had to wear a helmet. Reluctantly, but without great concern, Jacob departed sporting last year's model Thor brand bike helmet. (Nothing is cooler.) Though the humility might not have been because of Thor as much as it was being the only one wearing headgear. Gone for some twenty minutes already, Jacob's parents decided to take advantage of the free time and available television. Audrey's thesis is nothing more than a disciplinary tactic for marketing personal sponsors online that she'll later post on her website as workshop.

Unfortunately, the peaceful retreat is short lived. A sudden and somewhat firm knock at the door shatters the serenity. Audrey, a master of her environment, quickly finishes typing her last line, saves her progress, and bolts for the door while hurdling the ottoman on her way. Maybe out of some sort of maternal instinct or basic paranoia towards her son's recent expansion of his independence, Audrey reaches the door and rips it open expecting the worst.

Outside the door and standing at attention, two highly-decorated military officials accompanied by Dr. Walter Truax, centers the front stoop. Smiling as he speaks, Walter forces his eerie introduction, "And you must be Mrs. Bradley Simpson?"

Audrey unsurprisingly remarks, "Who the hell are you?"

"Forgive me, my name is Dr. Walter Truax. I'm a senior physician with the Medical Board of Trust."

"So?" Audrey leans her weight against the doorframe and crosses her right arm over the threshold.

"We need to ask your husband a few questions regarding his autopsy results." Walter exclaims.

"Sure." Audrey simply turns her head and yells out, "Bradley!"

Audrey turns back to her guests and sneers with distrust. After a short, tension flooded moment, Bradley emerges behind Audrey in the doorway.

"Yes, dear?" Bradley has his own way with words.

"I believe *these* are for you." Audrey points to Walter and his entourage before stepping aside to allow Bradley into the doorway.

"Oh. Why thank you, honey." Bradley gives his wife a sincere peck on the cheek. Audrey returns inside to her dissertation while Bradley takes the helm.

"Good afternoon, gentlemen. Welcome." Bradley's ostentatious side is in full-swing now.

"Dr. Simpson, my name is Dr. Walter Truax. This is General Dobbs and General Taylor." Walter playfully changes the subject, "She's quite the pistol, isn't she?"

"Who?" Bradley's pretty sure he knows to whom Walter is referring, but he decides to play along anyway.

"Your wife." Walter declares.

Bradley turns and looks inside at Audrey with grand affection and as nonchalantly as ever, he replies, "Ha, you better hope she doesn't have a pistol." Bradley then turns back to his visitors. " So? What can I do for you?"

"May I come inside?" Walter steps toward the doorway but Bradley doesn't budge.

"No. What can I do for you?" Bradley responds. Apprehensive conviction conjures insistency.

Walter is disheartened but yet somewhat impressed with Dr. Simpson's valor. He'll make for a prized aficionado. Dr. Truax quickly counters, "You can enlighten me on your findings the other day, Doctor. Or would you now rather be conspicuous?"

A familiar chill runs down Bradley's spine but he must stick to his guns. "My findings? A drunken man shot six people, three died from ricochets, and the shooter took his own life totaling ten in all. What more do you need to know?"

"So you're saying alcohol was the only thing you found inside the shooter's body?" Walter doesn't fear direct.

Bradley is becoming concerned that Dr. Truax knows more than he's admitting. He wonders if he should keep playing dumb or just invite Dr. Truax inside and try to get to the bottom of all this, but that would mean subjecting his house and family.

As if Bradley's fears and doubts were not great enough, Jacob and his friends suddenly appear over the hill heading in Bradley's direction. Flying down the street on their bikes, the four-some quickly turns into the driveway and brakes, sliding sideways and screeching to a halt. The boys hold back and stare in wonder at the military officials standing on the front doorstep. Surprisingly, Bradley actually catches a hint of nervousness on Walter's part. Like his secret visit was spoiled by Jacob and his friend's sudden arrival.

Dr. Truax sharply turns to Bradley and declares in a hushed but demanding voice, "I know what you've found, Doctor Simpson. As soon as you removed the pods, our courier signal quickly diminished. You are messing with unseen forces you cannot possibly comprehend. I urge you to keep what you know safely tucked away. For everyone's sake."

Dr. Truax turns and walks off of the front stoop with his silent protectors following close behind. Jacob and his friends remain in the driveway as they watch Dr. Truax walk passed and up to a silver sedan that's parked nearby in the street while the two Generals climb into the black SUV that's parked in the drive. The truck backs down the driveway and into the street before driving off behind the sedan. Both vehicles eventually disappear over the hill.

Jacob and his friends can't help but run over to Bradley and inquire about the recent visitors.

"Was *that* the government?" Jacob starts the interrogation.

"Are you being indicted, Mr. Simpson?" Jacob's friends help.

"Did you get fired?"

"Did you find Jimmy Hoffa?"

"Are you going to get concrete shoes?"

Bradley quickly intervenes, "All right, that's enough! You boys go home. Jacob, come inside. Now."

"But Dad!"

"Don't argue with me. We need to have a family discussion."

Bradley waits as Jacob moseys his way up the front steps and through the door.

Jacob's friends walk back to their bikes as the Simpson's front door closes behind them.

"Told you. He's being indicted."

"No. Witness protection."

"He'll be sleeping with the fishes by morning."

The boys laugh light-heartedly amidst their conspiracy theories before rallying the bikes and riding off into the sunset.

CHAPTER 5

A COLLEAGUE LOST

St. John's Medical Center shares its medical park with the County Coroner's Office along with various other administration buildings and offices of specialized practice.

Bradley always enters the north side of the park where the back lot allows direct access to his office and the examiner's lab. Though his house is modest, his beige with chrome trim Mercedes four-by-four reflects his more ostentatious side. Carefully approaching his parking space as usual, Bradley notices something different waits.

Detective Paige Dunbar leans against her "unmarked" car: charcoal colored, tinted windows, red lettering on the license plate. Paige wears her favorite sunglasses, a gray T-shirt tucked into black cargo pants, and her sidearm noticeably dangling from her hip. She actually looks really sexy.

Unfortunately, Bradley doesn't take into account the sexiness. He's suddenly worried that the detective waits to unravel more of his story. A direct contravention of Dr. Truax's warning. Dr. Simpson eases into his parking space hesitant to even exit the vehicle.

Bradley wonders if he should just throw the truck in reverse and make for his getaway when a warm engaging smile comes over Paige's face. Bradley turns off the engine and decides to step out and confront his company.

"Nice ride." Paige starts things off.

"Thank you, Detective. You too." Classic Bradley comeback.

Paige turns and looks at her '03 Crown Victoria then laughs. "Now I know you're being modest. Charm never begets you."

"Thank you, Detective." Bradley has her right where he wants her.

"Oh, call me Paige." Oops, maybe not. (Miss Dunbar is good.)

Bradley has no choice but to get to the point, "OK then, Paige. What can I do for you?"

"Well, Doctor." Paige's smile fades. She pushes herself up off the car. "You can tell me why three of the victim's bodies were taken to the Coroner's Office instead of your examination room?"

Bradley doesn't have to evade this question. "Honestly, I don't know. Maybe it was like you said, the gravity of six executive board members at the same place, at the same time. Maybe the others were just innocent bystanders."

"Maybe not." Detective Dunbar steps forward at Bradley. "Doctor, I need you to accompany me to the Coroner's Office. Immediately."

Dr. Simpson has always been intimidated by authority figures and their lone adverbs. He quickly complies. As they turn and make their way through the parking lot, Bradley can't help but walk with his head tilted downward while holding his hands behind his back.

"I'm not going to cuff you." Detective Dunbar exclaims. "Just walk." She pushes Bradley on the shoulder in playful retort.

Bradley relaxes enough to lower his hands but not enough to raise his head. A commuting doctor nearly runs him over with a four-door Audi. Bradley spins backwards from the passing car's inertia and into the waiting arms of Detective Dunbar. They share an awkward moment yet again.

"Something on your mind, Doctor?" Paige can tell Bradley is greatly distracted.

"I'm a married man." Bradley assumed their embrace was momentous.

Paige pushes Bradley back up. "That's not exactly what I had in mind. You seem distracted. Frightfully so, I might add."

"No. I just...didn't see him coming. That's all." Bradley continues on to the Coroner's Office while Paige pauses for a moment trying to dissect the good doctor's precariousness.

The detective catches up and as Bradley holds the door, she enters the office thanks to his act of chivalry. The doctor immediately follows.

The Coroner's Office greets visitors in a small waiting room where a sliding glass window allows the receptionist to appropriately direct. Bradley and Paige walk up to the glass and Bradley knocks on the window with the back of his forefinger to alert the receptionist, Valerie Dugan, of their presence. She rolls over and leans out of her office chair to slide open the window.

"Hey there, Val." Bradley being a frequent guest of the facility.

"Hey, Dr. Simpson, you old bloodhound. How's the tracking business?" Valerie is a kindred spirit in the family of forensic autonomy.

Bradley responds typically, "Oh, you know. The job never stops."

"Tell me about it." Valerie adjusts to a more personal curiosity, "How's Audrey and my little buddy, Jacob?"

"They're good. Driven by their adrenaline everyday. You know how it is." The good doctor doesn't often lie.

"Oh, I know." Valerie has frequented enough Christmas parties or summertime barbeques to vouch for his family's joviality. They engage in a taste of small talk before Valerie gets down to business. "So, what brings you in today? You're not in any trouble I hope." Valerie acknowledges Detective Dunbar standing there armed and voluptuous.

"No, this is Detective Paige Dunbar." Bradley replies. "We wanted to check on something."

Valerie responds somewhat curious, "OK. What?"

Bradley leans forward and almost whispers, "Who's on the floor today? Phil or Bryan?" Being Bryan is the new guy, Bradley has yet to place trust in him.

Valerie responds, "Phil."

Bradley straightens himself upright and calmly replies, "Oh, good. I just wanted to ask him a couple questions about the bodies that came in the other day."

Valerie calmly encourages, "Well, you know were to find him. Me casa a sue casa."

"Thanks, Val." Bradley enters the door directly left of the reception counter.

"Don't mention it, Dr. Simpson." Valerie continues working on her computer as she slides the window closed with one hand while maintaining her type with the other.

The doctor and the detective enter to a narrow hallway. Mainly office spaces or administrative departments, the hallway eventually leads to a large examining room that's not too dissimilar than that of Dr. Simpson's own lab.

Bradley opens the door and they both enter to find the Coroner, Dr. Phillip Grischow, standing with his back turned over one of three bodies that lie on separate examination tables and operating with extreme concentration. The blankets that cover the bodies have been pulled down beyond the torso. Oddly enough, Bradley doesn't see anything out of place and simply says, "What's up, Phil?"

Phil spins around wildly, surprised and scared half to death.

"Bradley? What the hell are you doing here?" Phil says. Not your conventional welcome, but a demanding conviction.

"Whoa, sorry. I didn't mean to startle you. I just wanted to ask you about the bodies they brought in Wednesday." Bradley can tell Phil's a little more high-strung than usual, even enough for concern.

"Yeah, what about them?" Phil turns a cold shoulder back to his work.

Bradley can't help but inquire about the coroner's three cadavers, "Are these them?"

"Yep." Phil works quickly and unsure of his fingers. He hurriedly probes what appears to be a bullet wound.

Bradley knows something is wrong and takes advantage of Phil's disengagement. He puts his arm out and signals Detective Dunbar to hold back while he approaches the target. Bradley slowly walks toward Phil while at the same time, Paige reaches down to her sidearm and unbuckles the holster. Paige clenches the pistol grip and waits in limbo for any impending occurrence. Bradley speaks inconspicuously as he advances. "Were they all victims of ricochets?"

"Yep." Phil still responds morbidly.

Bradley slowly makes his way to the other side of the operating table to admire Dr. Grischow's not so handiwork. The coroner uses surgical tweezers to crudely dig at the wound in the victim's right shoulder. Bradley impulses, "What are you doing?"

"Removing a bullet." Phil's dispassionate and almost robotic behavior concerns Bradley enough to cut to the chase.

"Phil? Are you all right?"

Phil doesn't even look up as he speaks to Bradley. "Yeah. Why?"

"I don't know. You just seem a little more distant than usual."

Sweat has begun to bead down Phil's forehead and his breathing is growing heavy from the scrutiny, "I'm fine."

"Then what the hell are you doing? You're not digging to China over here."

"I told you. I'm removing a bullet."

"Well neatness counts, Phil." Bradley experiences a moment of hesitation before instinctively blurting out, "Why were these bodies brought to you instead of me? How are they connected to the board members?"

Dr. Grischow doesn't respond, instead he quickens his pace. A nervous twitch takes over Phil's expressions. He shakes his head as if trying to regain vision after getting water in his eyes.

Bradley persists, "What are you hiding? Are you sure they were all victims of ricochets?"

Still no response. Detective Dunbar stands anxious to draw.

"Answer me. Were they all victims of ricochets?"

Suddenly calm, "I know of at least one for sure." Dr. Grischow retracts his tweezers from the wound firmly holding a compacted bullet in the tips of his utensil. He drops the slug into a stainless steel tray.

Bradley acknowledges the bullet, "Oh."

Bradley and Paige enjoy a sigh of relief, Paige especially, while Dr. Grischow continues, "Would you mind handing me some thread?" Phil motions to the surgical thread lying on the prop table behind Bradley. Bradley retrieves and hands Dr. Grischow the thread assuming it's to sew the wound. Phil takes the scalpel from the steel tray and slices off a section of thread. While prepping the needle, Phil finally breaks his monotony, "So, tell me? Why exactly are you pestering the hell out of me?"

Bradley admits, "Sorry, Phil. I just think there's more going on than a random shooting spree. We're wondering if these victims were innocent bystanders or intentionally targeted."

"Who's the other half of this we're?" Dr. Grischow offers Paige a menacing glance, but he isn't well aware of Detective Dunbar's fortitude.

Paige promptly strides toward the coroner exclaiming, "My name is Detective Paige Dunbar, Dr. Grischow, and I'm sure you wouldn't mind cooperating with us in this matter? Right?" Detective Dunbar stops a few yards short of the two doctors.

Dr. Grischow's eyes begin to twitch again. He tries to close his eyes and respond calmly, but he speaks through his gritted teeth saying, "Sure. Why not."

The detective maintains her discipline and agrees, "Good."

Meanwhile, Bradley has worked his way behind the operating tables and over to the other two bodies to investigate. Bradley surprises Phil again when he speaks, revealing his new whereabouts. "Where are the other bullet wounds?"

Phil quickly turns and approaches Bradley before replying, "I've already cleaned and sutured the wounds." Dr. Grischow grabs the blanket and pulls it up over the body.

Bradley comes right back. "Did you perform an autopsy?"

Dr. Grischow wavers, attempting to control his nerves as they create cerebral pulses that distort his focus. "I was about to."

Bradley goes for the jugular, "Phil? Pretend that I don't do the same thing for a living. These bodies have been here for days. You weren't preparing for any autopsies and you haven't cleaned any wounds. I would say that you're trying to cover your tracks, but I already examined the bodies and none of them show any signs of recent surgery. So that tells me these bodies didn't die from stray bullets."

Detective Dunbar chimes in, "Besides, you just finished cleaning a shoulder wound. I don't know of many fatal shoulder wounds."

"Phil?" Bradley leaves the ball in Dr. Grischow's court.

However, Dr. Grischow doesn't respond. His eyes and face convulse and his body begins to tremble.

Bradley drops his guard for concern of his friend. "Phil, what's wrong with you? You look like you're about to have a seizure. Did Truax do this to you?"

Dr. Grischow stops shaking long enough to look up at Bradley.

Bradley extends his arm and puts his hand on Phil's shoulder before softly speaking, "Phil, let me help you."

"You can't." Dr. Grischow suddenly reaches into his lab coat and pulls out the scalpel that he quietly concealed earlier. He slashes at Bradley's chest, left to right, and cuts a large gash from the mid ribs to the upper pectoral. Bradley quickly steps back and hunches his upper body over to try and withstand the pain, crossing his arms tightly over the chest to assist. Phil turns and grabs the stainless steel tray behind him and throws it at Detective Dunbar.

Paige grabs her gun and preps to aim as she watches Phil attack, but the incoming tray causes her to raise her arms in defense and miss the shot. Paige deflects the tray and its contents while Phil uses the opportunity to make another attempt on Bradley.

Dr. Grischow quickly turns and sets his hands on the operating table for leverage and hurdles himself over the table and corpse. His momentum crashes him directly into Bradley. Bradley falls to the floor and suffers another gash on his left arm in the process. Phil positions himself over Bradley, drops a knee down onto his chest, and raises the scalpel for the final blow.

With perfect timing, Detective Dunbar's well placed shot to the center of Dr. Grischow's back throws his body forward and on top of Bradley. As Phil falls, Bradley has to lean right in an attempt to avoid the incoming scalpel.

A still moment passes before Dr. Bradley Simpson rolls the coroner's body off of him in victory. Detective Dunbar remains poised in her triangular stance while smoke continues to rise from the muzzle of her sidearm.

Dr. Phillip Grischow is rolled onto his back, and though his paralyzed body is essentially done, Phil preserves enough life to offer Bradley a final message.

Still on the floor, Bradley leans over his friend and speaks first, "I'm sorry, Phil."

Phil stops him there, interrupting with a raspy, almost inaudible voice, "Bradley, get out of here. You have to get away from him. Take your family and go." Phil tries to muster more but chokes on his remaining thoughts and exhales. Dr. Phillip Grischow dies.

CHAPTER 6

SURPRISE AUTOPSY

Paramedics and police have now taken over The County Coroner's Office. Evidence is being gathered and medical respects are maintained around the four covered bodies in the room. Valerie Dugan speaks with investigators in an almost panic-stricken but yet passive manner. She suffers from a mild state of shock brought on by a brutal attack of which she was totally oblivious.

Dr. Bradley Simpson sits outside, topless, and in the back of an open ambulance. Two wraps of white gauze, one small and one large, encircle the doctor's chest and left bicep. Detective Paige Dunbar naturally leans on the back corner of the ambulance door observing the paramedic nurse our wounded hero back to health. Concern is soon replaced with admiration. Admiration is soon replaced with curiosity.

Paige asks of him, "What is it that you're not telling me?"

Dr. Simpson looks up slowly, occupied by the thought that he can't keep his secret forever, but still invoked by man's most common reaction when the proverbial jig is up: play dumb. Bradley's response, "Huh?"

Paige Dunbar has long aspired to be a force to reckon with and tolerance has proven to be her greatest asset, but direct proves just as useful. "Don't play dumb with me, Doctor. I can read between the lines. You asked Dr. Grischow if Truax did that to him. Who is Truax?"

"He's nobody. Just a former colleague of Grischow's." Bradley doesn't often lie because he's known to dig himself into holes that prove hard to clamber.

Detective Dunbar returns prepared, "Yeah? First we have the massacre of six executive board members from the largest prescription drug company in the world, all at the same place, all at the same time. Then three innocent bystander's bodies were conveniently misplaced while no report was ever issued to authorities, media, or even the families. And now this? The County Coroner goes off the deep end after the three bystanders were found in his possession and he tries murdering you in an attempt to conceal it? You mention some Truax guy being responsible and then you tell me he was just a colleague? Don't tell me it's all a coincidence. What are you hiding? Why won't you help me connect the dots?"

Stunned, Dr. Simpson can't think of a witty comeback. Detective Dunbar hit the nail right on the head with her observation. Maybe Bradley realizes that if he is going to defeat this evil, he's going to need help as well. Bradley sighs in relief and decides to divulge his secret to the detective.

Detective Dunbar sits down next to Bradley in the ambulance and listens while the doctor catches her up to speed.

Meanwhile elsewhere... A Live Action News report is set for broadcast and Abra Malone is on the scene. The cameraman uses his fingers to count down from five before signaling Abra on when to begin.

"This is Abra Malone reporting for Live Action News from the city's Financial District. The brainchild of late founder, Tony Vicelli, Magnus Medical Distribution Corporation officially liquidated its assets a little less than an hour ago. Consolidated in the late eighties, Magnus will now be split back into its five, original, government financed organizations, ending the sway of the world's most powerful drug conglomerate. Government officials on behalf of each organization, represented their company's interests in sustaining regulatory allocation. Now recognized as Invas Research Facility, Pharmtec Laboratories, New Youth Compounds, N.E.T.I. Pharmaceuticals, and Equinox, the privately funded, government owned organizations will have to maintain their own records of capital while distribution will be managed through the FDA's and American Medical Association's authorized shipping centers. Each organization will continue to manufacture their specialized compounds, including medicine for indigestion and acidity from Invas, medicine for blood pressure and liver disease from Pharmtec, pills for erectile dysfunction and low testosterone from New Youth, treatments for depression and mental illness from N.E.T.I., and drugs for muscular dystrophy and multiple sclerosis from Equinox. Though insurance companies assured people that their medical premiums won't go up as a result of this dissolution, many are still concerned about the future of their prescription plans. What started as the city's worst crime in decades, has quickly led to the city's greatest stock frenzy in history. And as the concerns escalate, so does the assumption that prices will shortly follow. With continuing coverage for Live Action News, this is Abra Malone."

Long story short, the distribution of the bugs has begun.

Back at the Coroner's Office... Detective Paige Dunbar sits speechless from the newfound knowledge of Bradley's conspiracy theory.

The detective eventually responds, "So, you're telling me these bugs are in us all the time just waiting to execute their program?"

"Yes." Bradley admits.

Paige continues, "And there's no way of stopping them?"

"I don't know yet." The good doctor doesn't often lie.

"What are you going to do?" Detective Dunbar sets the next question in motion, but an unknown authority figure appears around the side of the ambulance and halts the investigative progress. Their enemies don't go by the book.

Calmly but directly, the authority figure presents his introduction, "Dr. Bradley Simpson? My name is Chief Inspector Dempsey. I need to ask a favor of you?"

"What is it, Inspector?" For Bradley, curiosity is an incision waiting to be made.

"No report was ever filed in regards of the deceased. We need you to identify the bodies. I realize that you've had a traumatic day, but there's no one else. Please?" Oddly, Inspector Dempsey seems personally troubled by the impending autopsy results and therefore driven by his concern. He doesn't express some nonchalant sense of duty to implore finality, instead he almost fears the unknown truth of one or all of the victims.

Bradley's curiosity and own sense of duty causes his response, "Absolutely, Inspector. Any way I can help."

Paige quickly interrupts, "What? Wait. No, you need to rest. You shouldn't even be here anyways, you should be in the hospital."

Bradley bypasses the detective's advice and reconfirms. "I'll do it."

"Thank you, Doctor." And as simple as that, Inspector Dempsey turns and disappears beyond the side of the ambulance well aware that his objective had been reached and completed. (Hook, line, and sinker.)

Bradley picks himself up and remarks chauvinistically, "Well, duty calls." He puts his sliced up, blood-soaked shirt back on.

However, Detective Dunbar's dumbfounded look catches the good doctor's attention.

"What?" Bradley can be so good at his work that it blinds him.

Paige enlightens him, "What's the matter with you? You have two gaping wounds on your body and you let yourself get coerced into going back to work? Look at yourself for crying out loud."

"Hey, it's what I do." Bradley then moves in close to Paige and whispers in her ear, "Besides, I need to know what was in Phil's head. He wasn't a murderer."

Detective Dunbar suddenly realizes why Bradley accepted the

inspector's favor so eagerly. Dr. Simpson would make for a great detective.

Many hours later... Bradley stands over a clipboard jotting down his results. The opaque white surgical gloves offer little obstruction to his designations.

Our unsung hero works wounded and alone, putting truth above all else in hopes of defeating some crazy ass scientist who wants to put microscopic robots in our bodies for reasons of playing puppeteer with our remedial dependencies. In a word: Dedicated.

The identification and pathological diagnosis is complete.

First bystander: Terra Reinstad. Terra's body displays no signs of a gunshot wound. Without an identifiable entrance or exit point, the autopsy concludes that the victim suffered a massive, panic in-duced heart attack. Three separate pods were all found inside heart valves, the aortic valve, the mitral valve, and the pulmonary vein to be exact. A sudden and simultaneous surge of electrical output from the pods effectively closed these valves and stopped the blood flow to and from the heart.

Terra was meant to be an innocent bystander that day. She was meant to be at that exact place, at that exact time, so that when the pods were activated during the few brief moments of the shooting spree, her body would suddenly fall to the floor and everybody would assume a stray bullet was to blame. Terra's toxicology report came back negative, but her DNA report delivered curious results. Terra Reinstad apparently shares a DNA match with the late, Dr. Charles Mendel, the original developer behind Neurolex. The most peculiar thing is that even though Dr. Mendel supposedly died from a gunshot wound as well, Bradley never found a bullet in his body either.

Second bystander: Saria Zehata. Saria's body also shows no signs of a gunshot wound. However, no pods were found in either her heart or her brain. Upon further investigation, and the extreme veining of Saria's bloodshot eyes, the autopsy report concludes that the victim was asphyxiated.

But how? Saria was sitting alone at the table in a wide-open diner. Nobody else complained of difficulties breathing. Saria's neck displays no bruising or signs of strangulation. Bradley had to dig pretty deep to discover the culprits.

Hidden well inside the primary bronchi, Bradley finds his largest specimens yet. Two pods, roughly the size of quarters and easily containing millions of individual bugs, aggravated the inner-lining of the bronchial passages and caused them to contract and collapse around the pods, thus cutting off air to the lungs. These particular pods appear to be an old, clunky, and more frightening version of a new dominant technology. Saria must've been exposed to the medication for some time now.

Her toxicology report also came back negative, but the DNA results were more disturbing than curious. Saria was obviously Dr. Mumahd Zehata's wife. Married a little more than five years, Mumahd and Saria were expecting their first child. Saria was over three weeks pregnant.

Third bystander: Merrill Broussard. Merrill is apparently the only victim that sustained a gunshot wound. The quarter-sized hole in his right shoulder is the same that Dr. Grischow was so aggressively probing earlier. Though no exit wound is present, Bradley fears that was the intention. What if the bullet was meant for distribution, not execution? Conveniently severing the subclavian vein and presenting a direct route to the right atrium, the bullet's trajectory and endpoint could've allowed countless attackers to enter the bloodstream. A ricochet is not likely that accurate.

Bradley's worst fears are realized when he finds fragments of broken robots within the wound that are now part of a microscopic debris field where the bullet shattered on impact. The same shattered slug that Dr. Grischow eventually removed.

Autopsy report concludes that the victim died from electrocution. The massive chain of burn marks that led to Merrill's heart suggests an electrical output of over one thousand volts and potentially eight individual pods. This gross overload of pods, and the lack of pods anywhere else in his body, proves that Merrill was not regimented but outright attacked. The bullet housed and later released billions of bugs within the host bystander.

Toxicology report shows the victim was fond of brandy and barbiturates, but not in large quantities. DNA results are as expected, Merrill obviously shares a bloodline with the late CEO of the former Magnus Cooperation, Eugene Broussard. Though traces of Tyler Vaughn's DNA were also discovered, it's only because the bullet passed through his upper torso before it impacted Merrill. (Coincidence?)

Final victim: Dr. Phillip Grischow. Bradley found five pods implanted in Phil's body. Three were in his brain: the cerebellum, frontal lobe, and temporal lobe. One was on his optic nerve. And one was in his tricuspid valve between the right atrium and ventricle.

Autopsy report concludes that the victim died from a gunshot wound to the upper left side of his torso. The bullet passed upwards through the ribs and left lung before exiting mere inches below the clavicle.

Phil's behavior leading up to the attack is what lays on Bradley's mind though. The pod on his optic nerve explained the eye twitching and blurred vision. The loss of self-control caused by the pods in his brain made sense since it strongly resembled the autopsy of the assailant in the blue hooded sweatshirt. But the final pod, placed alone in the heart valve, raises a red flag. The pod almost seems as a fail-safe. In the event that Phil didn't go through with his mission, it would've shut down his heart.

Toxicology report was negative and the DNA results were conclusive but irrelevant in connection to the other victims.

The hardest part is that Bradley has to take the responsibility of telling Phil's wife that he was dead. After all, Truax wasn't Grischow's former colleague, Bradley was.

Dr. Bradley Simpson now realizes the gravity of this massacre. The execution was performed in a manner that ownership of Magnus was not passed to the next of kin or in accordance to the primary beneficiaries of the victim's will. Bradley has to use the process of elimination in order to discover who's to benefit the most from splitting Magnus apart. He decides to take a stand. Bradley chooses to investigate the bloodline of the victims, starting with the first victim, Eugene Broussard.

Merrill Broussard needed to be shot and therefore implanted with pods. His body didn't already house bugs waiting to execute their program. Why? What about him created the immunity? What did he know? What did he do for a living?

CHAPTER 7

FULL-CONTACT COMMUTE

It was a long day. My good friend and former colleague tried murdering me today. My sexy tomboy sidekick put a bullet through
his back in my defense. I performed autopsies on four of the most
medically tampered bodies I've ever seen. And my story is apparently all over the eleven o'clock news. It's certainly all over the
radio.

Bradley drives home from work thinking about his recent pre-
dicament. Despite the pressing news on the radio about the County
Coroner being the latest death in a string of tragic events and how
Bradley again identified the victims, the lavish comfort of his ride
makes the atmosphere quite serene. The Mercedes SUV glides over
the road like an ice skater might on the rink, unlike the teeter-totter
effect comparable to a pickup truck with no weight in the bed. The
dark remoteness of the evening highway jostles the mind into creating metaphysical confrontations to heighten awareness. Whether
the thoughts are for relaxation or worry, the construct is the comfort. (Sanctuary through isolation).

Occasionally, Bradley must also share his tranquility with others. The dual glare of an approaching vehicle's headlights disrupts
his thought process. He diverts his attention to the rearview mirror.

The headlights quickly get larger despite Bradley's excessive speed. Most passers switch lanes and though it's not raining, Bradley must turn on his wipers to deflect spray from the wet road. However, this vehicle appears to close in and ride Bradley's bumper. Bradley's second reaction is to check his speed in case it's the police, and sure enough, his speed is excessive.

Unfortunately, the police never perform a P.I.T. maneuver without flashing their lights first to attempt a pullover. The sudden jolt fully awakens Bradley from his intellectual trance. He jerks the steering wheel trying to maintain control of the SUV. The four-wheel drive handles nicely.

Once corrected, Bradley glances through the rearview mirror again to access his attacker and notices the unknown vehicle line up for another bump. Bradley's natural reaction is to stomp down on the accelerator. The five-point-two liter engine of the Mercedes revs to its max, thrusting the utility vehicle forward and creating separation from the oncoming threat.

Bradley can tell from the dark outline of the vehicle that it is not a police cruiser. The smooth sheen reflecting off of the vehicle's roof reveals no lights are mounted on top brackets. It appears to be some type of four-door luxury sedan. The sedan's headlights pollute the details from Bradley's point of view.

The two automobiles leave tunnels of dew in their wake as they race down the dark, wet highway. The unknown vehicle attempts to pass Bradley on several occasions, but the reflection off the Mercedes' mirrors tips Bradley on when and where to move. The unknown vehicle knocks at Bradley's rear bumper the entire time.

Occasionally gaining separation, Bradley maintains good leverage over his pursuer. As Bradley once again observes the unknown vehicle move in for another P.I.T. maneuver, he suddenly gets a radical idea.

Bradley cuts over and aligns his SUV directly in front of the sedan and abruptly stomps on the brake. The Mercedes halts while the momentum of the unknown vehicle causes a chain reaction.

The high-speed impact bounces the rear end of Bradley's Mercedes on top of the sedan's hood while the force drives the sedan under the SUV till its roof gets pinned under the rear tires. Under such speed and momentum, the weight of Bradley's Mercedes crushes down on the sedan. After the roof and windshield of the unknown vehicle collapse, the Mercedes smashes back down on the hood and regains traction. The SUV drives off not only immobilizing the unknown vehicle, but also destroying its hood and entire engine compartment in the process. The unknown sedan lies dead in its tracks while the Mercedes is barely even scratched.

Bradley speeds off into the night with part of his rear bumper slightly dangling from the panel, very much ready to make it home and share this most recent experience.

The time is eleven-fifty-three p.m. The upper middle-class neighborhood rests peacefully predisposed for the workday ahead. The stillness of the night is dramatically shaken as a Mercedes SUV squeals into its driveway and then screeches to a halt.

Bradley jumps out of his vehicle and rushes up to the house. As Bradley unlocks the door and hurries inside, Audrey, brandishing her three-fifty-seven snub-nosed revolver, quickly descends the second story stairwell and greets him. Since Bradley effectively woke the entire neighborhood with his reckless parking job before entering the house, Audrey automatically assumed he was a threat.

Bradley reacts as he should, "Whoa, shit!"

Audrey responds, "For crying out loud, Bradley. What in the hell is wrong with you?" Audrey retracts her pistol in relief. "You scared the shit out of me."

"Uh, likewise."

"Are you alright? What's wrong?" Audrey pleads.

Bradley engages his anxiety. "We have to leave. Tonight."

Audrey disengages, "No. Why?"

"Someone just tried to kill me. I don't know who it was, but they seemed awfully determined to run me off the road."

"Oh my god, again? Are you all right? What happened?" Audrey asks.

Bradley continues on explaining the car chase, how he slammed on the brakes, and finally smashed the front end of an unknown sedan. And this is all after Phil tried to murder him earlier.

"What kind of car was it?" Audrey finally asks.

"I don't know. Some kind of luxury car."

"Oh, like the one your guest arrived in the other day?" Audrey has no problem pointing out the obvious.

"Yep. Pretty much." Neither does Bradley.

Audrey acts surprisingly perplexed. "Oh? So you know it was Truax?"

"Well, I figured. I don't know of anyone else who wants to kill me." Bradley always did have a way with words. "We need to get somewhere safe."

Audrey isn't so easily persuaded. She flexes the family muscle, "Absolutely not. If that man wants a problem, he can come and find one. In the meantime, Dr. Simpson, your son is trying to sleep. So I suggest you mellow out, and we can scrutinize the situation in the morning. Sound categorical?"

Bradley's response, "Ah, I love you."

Audrey's response, "You damn well better."

Audrey puckers her lips and offers Bradley a kiss. She doesn't raise her hand and blow the kiss his way, she just demonstrates her affection and returns upstairs still packing heat.

Irrevocably, Audrey's steel will depends on Bradley for stimulation while Bradley's overactive paranoid imaginative goal of perfection relies on Audrey for attenuation. Some might call it contradictory. Most just call it meant to be.

Bradley stands alone in his living room. The night has suddenly become calm thanks to Audrey's grit. Bradley takes a step toward the stairwell to conclude his long evening when his cell phone suddenly rings.

Bradley quickly, yet apprehensively, answers the unknown caller. "Hello?"

"I warned you of the consequences for digging too deep. I'm sure you'll come to terms with your options, Dr. Simpson. Sleep well." Click.

CHAPTER 8

BIRTH OF A DETECTIVE

Eugene Windsor Broussard was born in Montpelier, Vermont. The large built, six-foot-four business tycoon didn't actually grow his beard until he came to the big city. His predecessor and father however, André Broussard, came to America from Paris, France where he was accepted into the Yale School of Medicine. Young Eugene spent his youth in the shadow of André's success. Eugene attended the best schools and received the finest recommendations. Basically, he was born into it.

André opened his first pharmacy in 1945. Aptly named Broussard's, it was just four months after receiving his Physical Doctrine that André broke ground on his legacy. The money leased to create his business or to attend Yale is still to this day, unknown. Once established however, André branched out and opened small pharmacies all across the county. Before long, he was able to establish his corporation and set his birthright. (First state, then nation.)

Unfortunately in 1978, André Broussard died of pneumonia. His untimely death would leave over sixty-five percent of the Broussard Industry's shares to his only child, Eugene.

There is no medical record of Eugene Broussard. He apparently was born within the grounds of the Broussard estate and delivered by the nursemaid. No baby book, no footprint, and no lock of hair.

Eugene's mother unfortunately died while giving birth.

André had traveled back to Paris for a well deserved vacation from the pressures of an entrepreneur's life when during his visit, André met and fell in love with a young woman by the name of Calista Velour. Three months later, they married and set off for America. Eugene was born one year after.

Eugene's inheritance came as a shock to him. The love/hate relationship between father and son left an ill will at the time of André's death. Eugene was elated to lash out against the legacy responsible for desecrating his desire for family values.

Eugene sought independent buyers that would agree to purchase individual pharmacies while allowing Eugene a small percentage of the profits. He opportunely gained on both fronts.

Concluding the liquidation and dissolution of the Broussard trademark, Eugene actually invested his fortune into the strategy of a man that he met at a trade show, Tony Vicelli. Though dimly devised, the ideology behind Magnus Distribution Corporation motivated Eugene to bond a partnership, a partnership that would prove to be his fate.

Merrill Broussard is too, an enigma. He has no county, city, or state record of ever being born. There is no record on who his parents were, where he grew up, or how he even became educated. The anonymity of Merrill's repute resembles that of Eugene's clandestinely noble birth. Other than the DNA match from the autopsies, a few newspaper articles are the only proof that either of them even existed. But unlike Eugene, Merrill's nameplate did not echo through inheritance. (Runs in the family?)

The fact that Merrill's record has been so conveniently nonexistent, implies that he was either an adopted orphan, raised by wolves, or it has all been deemed classified.

One thing is for certain. Though seemingly a bystander, Merrill was an intended target at the diner. Therefore, he must've stood to gain something from that conference meeting.

So far, this is all the intelligence that Detective/Dr. Bradley Simpson could gather. Bradley slept relatively well, given his terrifying high-speed chase from the night before. He woke to the sound of Jacob's favorite cartoons and to the smell of bacon. Some might say that waking up to the smell of bacon makes for the best morning in the world. Waking up to the smell of coffee came in at a close second. (Arguably.)

Bradley, fashioning his favorite robe, happily descends the second story stairwell eager to acknowledge his family and his breakfast.

Jacob lies on the living room carpet watching TV. He rests stomach down with his elbows dug into the carpet so that his hands and arms can keep his head propped up. He occasionally bends his knees and legs backwards carelessly pedaling the air behind him.

Bradley's first impulse is to say, "There's furniture."

Jacob's first impulse is to reply, "I know."

Audrey stands in the kitchen cooking breakfast. The dazzling crackle of the boiling oil as it cooks the bacon in the skillet has an almost exhilarating comfort, sort of like the sound of falling water. Bradley is hypnotically drawn to his wife and the bacon.

"Good morning, dearest." Bradley conveys his affection with a peck on Audrey's cheek.

"Good morning, sleepyhead." Audrey smooches in return without removing her attention from the stovetop.

Bradley realizes her critique of his punctuality by noticing the digital clock in the kitchen. It reads 11:14 a.m. Bradley's biological clock usually doesn't allow him to sleep past eight, nine. It was a good night's rest.

Unfortunately, Audrey's Sunday morning over easy ambiance was not an accident. She gathered her strengths to set the chessboard (breakfast table) accordingly. As her two boys, Jacob and Bradley, take their seats at the kitchen table, Audrey unveils her motive.

"So? I noticed the truck this morning. Doesn't look good." Though the Mercedes was barely even scratched last night, the disconnected rear bumper that hangs slightly away from the frame still offers a small cosmetic blemish.

Bradley comes back, "Well, I told you..."

Audrey interrupts to keep the momentum in the conversation, "And that's what I'm wondering about. This Truax guy, who claims to be on the Medical Board of Trust, just shows up at our house out of the blue to question you about your autopsy results, and then the next thing you know he's trying to run you off the road? You mind telling me what's going on?"

Bradley's response, "Well, I didn't want to worry you."

"You kind of failed at that objective last night. I think we've come to that need-to-know basis." Audrey stays on point.

A wave of fear rushes over Bradley. He's concerned about letting his family onto his secret and breaking the superstitious cover that ignorance is blissful. Will informing them, involve them?

Bradley takes pride in their strong family values. He overcomes his fears and entrusts his family with the truth. "First off, he's not with the Medical Board of Trust..."

...After listening for about ten minutes, Audrey and Jacob stare at Bradley in disbelief. Literally, they don't believe him.

Bradley's complex and overly imaginative story doesn't seem very plausible. Jacob toys around with the idea of having a bunch of tiny bugs operating his bodily functions. He asks his father if they'll allow him to see through walls, run faster than a speeding bullet, and leap tall buildings in a single bound. (The usual stuff.)

Audrey is more scientifically skeptical that acids in the body would dissolve the bugs, therefore making the engineering and networking capabilities impossible.

Either way, Bradley shares his idea that all of the victims were sequentially removed from the inheritance of Magnus's shares and his plan to track the bloodline of the three bystanders for any correlations.

Thus, Detective Bradley Simpson is born. Though Audrey is actually the one who went online to dig up any information they could find on Merrill Broussard, Terra Reinstad, and Saria Zehata. She obviously profiled Merrill first. Once the information is collected, Bradley will then set off on his quest.

But since they couldn't find anything substantial to go on, Bradley resorted to checking the phone book. To his luck though, there were only four Broussard's listed: two lived in apartments, one lived in moderate income housing, and one lived high in the foothills were the lease on property is anything but cheap. The address listed reads: Broussard, Mimi. 41295 Sycamore Grove.

Who the hell is Mimi Broussard? Our hero must find out.

However, Bradley must first head somewhere else before conquering the foothills: Phillip Grischow's house.

Even though his wife Carol, and two daughters Nicole and Lindsey, have already learned of Phil's death, Bradley still feels personally compelled to offer his condolences.

The Grischow house is located within the Country Club Estates. It's not a gated community, but visitors do have to check-in at the guard station upon arrival.

Bradley states his purpose and proceeds down the lane. The modern development boasts large, well-kept yards with grand oak and elm trees as their accents. The lane flows directly into the Country Club where members engage in recreations like golfing, swimming, tennis, and even fine dining.

Bradley pulls up to a large, off-white house. The concrete driveway and approach lead to the front stoop where two concrete pillars brace the entryway roof. High arched and half-moon shaped windows span the façade while most of the community's backyards come equipped with Florida rooms that overlook the golf course's lush fairways.

Bradley gets out of his truck and walks up to the front door before pressing the bell for admittance. After a brief moment, a little blonde face swishes the curtain on the door aside to peer out at the visitor. She evaluates Bradley and disappears behind the curtain again, probably to seek out a parental figure who can allow strangers proper admission. After a few more brief moments, Carol Grischow answers the door.

Offering a hug with humble apathy, Bradley acknowledges the degree of Carol's loss.

Carol accepts and reciprocates in the form of, "Thank you, Bradley. I'm glad you stopped by. Please, come in." Carol gestures for Bradley to enter and he proceeds indoors.

Once in the door, the little blonde face that originally alerted the house to his presence, quickly meets Bradley. It's Phillip's youngest daughter, Lindsey. She always welcomes Bradley the same way, "Hi, Doctor Bradley."

Bradley responds, "Hi, Lindsey. You're getting bigger and bigger every time I see you."

"That's cause I'm four now," answers Lindsey.

Bradley takes time to preserve the child's innocence, "Wow! You're growing up so fast."

However, Carol can't dance around the subject. She quickly intervenes, "People have been stopping by all day, offering their condolences. I know that's why you're here. I can appreciate the gesture, Bradley, but I need answers. What happened to my husband?"

"Is that why Doctor Bradley is here? To find daddy?" asks Lindsey.

The only response that Bradley can come up with is, "I don't know what to say?"

Carol and Lindsey both begin their sentences at the same time, but Lindsey's comment overpowers. "We can help you find him."

Bradley is heartbroken by the virtuousness of a non-conversant youth. The realization of her father's death might take years to understand.

Carol responds as any responsible mother would, "Lindsey. Go upstairs and play with your sister."

"But she's online." Lindsey defies.

"Just go." Carol insists.

"Fine." Lindsey stomps out of the room depleted of her candidness.

Carol turns her attention back to Bradley. "You performed the autopsy. Tell me what happened."

Bradley treads lightly, "It's hard to explain. Was Phil's behavior a little strange leading up to the incident?"

"He seemed confused. Unsure of what he was doing, where he was going, or what he was even working on. Please Bradley, just tell me." Carol beckons.

"I found several anomalies inside Phil's body. Robots were implanted in his brain that appeared to interrupt nerve receptors and create the basic symptoms of dementia. I'm not quite sure how. When I found him, he almost seemed lost, but yet driven. Driven at either finding something or hiding something..." A thought suddenly interrupts Bradley's diagnosis. "...Carol? Had Phil met or interacted with anyone unusual, or different? Did anyone come to visit him?" Bradley lays down the initial groundwork.

Carol informs him, "Now that you mentioned it, I did see him shaking hands with someone outside the house a couple weeks ago. It was strange. Phil pulled out to go to work, and this man just pulled in front of our house to confront him. I guess it seemed harmless enough."

"Did Phil ever mention this man?" Bradley asks.

"No."

Bradley continues, "What kind of car was he driving?"

"I don't know, some sort of luxury car. Like a Lincoln or a Buick." Carol's observation hits home.

Dr. Walter Truax had obviously gotten to Phil first. But Why? Why was Phil a threat? Why was he an asset?

"Did Phil tell you what he was working on at the time?" asks Bradley.

Carol answers, "He said he was responsible for the three bystanders from the shooting spree. That's about it."

Bradley acts confused, "He said he was responsible for them? Responsible for what?"

"I don't know. The autopsies I guess. Why?" Carol doesn't see anything wrong with this scenario.

Bradley explains, "I usually examine the bodies before they're sent to Phil for the official report. In addition, the official report requires judicial approval before its contents can be accurately released to family, media, the press, stuff like that. I guess it's just unorthodox for Phil to have autonomy over the results."

"What do you think that means?" Carol wonders.

Since Bradley has already released his secret conspiracy theory to his family and Detective Dunbar, he figures letting Carol know for the sake of closure wouldn't hurt anything. "I think it means that Phil was bought off. Bought off to keep something covered-up," replies Bradley.

Carol inquires, "Keep *what* covered-up?"

Bradley divulges his secret.

Ten minutes later...

Carol responds, "Bradley? Are you making this up?"

Bradley turns and throws his arms in the air in a frustrated tantrum, "Why doesn't anyone believe me?"

Maybe because that's the curse of playing whistle blower: Validity of doubt.

Carol maintains her solace, "I'm sorry, Bradley. It's just not your everyday theory. It sounds too much like science fiction."

Bradley goes into detective mode, "Well, I have a lead on one of the victims. I'm headed there now. Maybe something will turn up that'll help me get to the bottom of all this. I'll be in touch."

"Thanks, Bradley. Bye" Carol walks over to the door and holds it open while Bradley makes his exit.

Bradley usually waits to speak with both Lindsey and Nicole before leaving. Bradley and Nicole have always gotten along because Nicole is Jacob's friend. Being they're both in the same grade and class together, their parents have carpooled for each other in the past, but Nicole doesn't seem to have any interest in Bradley's visit.

And that's when it hits Bradley...

At first, Carol was desperately concerned for truth on her husband, Bradley tells her, she doesn't believe him, and then she nonchalantly whisks him out the door. She knew Phil attacked him and she didn't even ask if he was all right. Meanwhile Nicole, the one who usually comes running to ask him about Jacob, is nowhere to be found.

Bradley ponders to himself as he leaves, "I wonder if they think *I* did it?"

CHAPTER 9

BROUSSARD ESTATE

The foothills surrounding the metropolis make for a well-established hideaway for the successful entrepreneur types, as well as many of their secured facilities. Thick vegetation and steep hillsides make this area an engineering nightmare, hence the expensive lease on land.

Back in the early twenties, a logging company was contracted to excavate the foothills for governmental development. Since a majority of the trees timbered were sycamores, the pathway was dubbed Sycamore Grove. Only the super wealthy, who later began inhabiting the area, could afford the four-wheel drive vehicles or the gas to power them to even get up these hills.

Thankfully, global marketing incentives can allow our hero an affordable all-terrain class of this mobility: score one for the good guys!

According to the Internet's database of personal records, Mimi Broussard, 41295 Sycamore Grove, actually runs her own non-profit organization for the education and development of homeless children. That's why her address, along with her phone number, is accessible in the book. It shows no record of Mimi ever being married or having children.

Maybe Merrill was an adopted orphan after all. Bradley must first talk with Mimi to confirm.

But before that, Bradley must find the damn place. There are no mailboxes or discernable addresses out here that mark which dirt road is which. Bradley must take a guess, ascend into no-man's land, and hope for the best.

Following a few failed choices of dirt roads leading to locked gates, Bradley picks an inconspicuously overgrown grass pathway marked by two lines that indicate tire tracks. The pathway turns upward while it doglegs right, through the tree line, and into the forest.

After about a hundred yards, the forest pathway opens to a large clearing. An old and unkempt estate looms in its center while the rusty iron fence that guards its perimeter rests slightly open. Two brick pillars reinforce the gate. The pillar on the right bears a large concrete block with the engraving: BROUSSARD.

Our hero has done it!

Bradley pulls up to the fence and gets out. He decides to walk from this point.

The residence doesn't appear to have accommodated any recent occupants. There's no cars parked outside. Large patches of weeds and ivy blanket the driveway, the walkways, and the estate itself. The high shrill that the gate hinges make when Bradley enters, suggest oxidation and a lack of grease for probably a couple years now. Bradley slowly approaches the front entrance wondering if this is just another dead end. He'll soon find out that it's much more than that.

To Bradley's surprise, the doorbell actually rings when he presses it, offering a low, dull chime like church bells striking the hour. After a few disappointing seconds and again to Bradley's surprise, someone answers the door.

A heavyset, gray haired woman opens the door. Wearing a rainbow-striped muumuu, she delivers no introduction or greeting. She just stares at Bradley and waits for his lead.

Following an uncomfortable pause, Bradley finally speaks.

"Um, excuse me, ma'am? My name is Dr. Bradley Simpson. I'm the Medical Examiner at St. John's Medical Center. I was wondering if I might be able to speak with Mimi Broussard?"

The old woman plainly responds, "You're able. Speak."

"Are you Mimi?" Bradley asks. His intake isn't as fast as his SUV's.

Mimi breaks it down for him, but not without having a bit of fun first.

"Not quite as sharp as your tools, eh Doctor? Yes, I'm Mimi. But only so you can take that puzzled look off your face."

Mimi's witty spitfire personality has certainly left Bradley in the dust. He still hasn't abandoned his speechlessness. Mimi continues, "I guess not. What can I do for you, Doctor?"

Bradley stammers over his vernacular, "I, uh. Um. Oh yeah..."

"...Welcome back." Mimi interrupts Bradley's struggling intellectual mechanics with a playful impatience.

Bradley eventually continues, "Thanks. I'm the one who performed the autopsy on Merrill."

Mimi releases a sigh before revealing, "I know, Doctor. I watch the news."

Bradley keeps pace, "I was wondering if you can tell me his relation to Eugene?"

"Of course, Eugene was my brother." Mimi calmly responds.

"So Eugene was Merrill's uncle?" Bradley is starting to find light at the end of this tunnel.

Mimi replies, "Well, not exactly." (Maybe not.)

"Huh?"

"I adopted Merrill when he was only four months old. He was orphaned when his parents where both gunned down in their home. Merrill was asleep upstairs. The police later found him." Mimi informs.

Bradley is more lost now than before. "So then if Merrill wasn't related to Eugene, why was he at The Avenue that day?"

Mimi doesn't respond. Instead she looks around the premise before unobtrusively offering, "Please, Dr. Simpson, let us go inside and talk civilly." Mimi motions for Bradley to enter.

Bradley also turns and checks the perimeter before entering. He steps inside the neglected estate and the door slowly creaks closed behind him.

The Broussard estate must've been quite the sight in its heyday. Marble flooring, two fine-finished mahogany stairwells ascending to the second story, dozens of magnificent art pieces along with various antiquities, brilliant chandeliers, and high cathedral ceilings trimmed with polished rosewood. (All now covered in dust.)

Mimi leads Bradley through the central reception area and left into the kitchen where she makes her way over to the cupboards and begins shuffling about. The distinct clink of teacups echoes through the wooden breakfront. Mimi turns to Bradley. "Would you care for tea?"

"Yes, please." Bradley accepts.

Mimi takes two teacups down and makes her way over to the stovetop and kettle.

Bradley takes a stool at the kitchen island.

While Mimi prepares the tea, she begins, "Merrill was never supposed to be at that god-awful diner. In fact, I didn't even know he'd come back into town until I heard about the shooting spree. Eugene always wanted Merrill to be involved with his corporation. He would offer him positions in the company, shares of the stock. It would drive me nuts. Merrill was all for it, of course, it was big money. I just didn't want to see him give up his career that he worked so hard for to go after the easy money. It seemed rootless."

Bradley chimes in, "What was his career?"

"He was a tactical software designer for the Department of Defense." Mimi stuns her audience with this little factoid.

Bradley tries desperately not to shit a brick as Mimi brings him the tea. So Merrill was in fact, a classified adopted orphan.

Mimi sets the cups down and takes the stool across the island from Bradley.

"Thank you." The good doctor responds. He takes the cup with a slight shake in his hands. The newfound knowledge of just how deep this cover-up goes starts to test his nerves.

Mimi resumes, "Eugene had named Merrill as his primary beneficiary in the will. So in the event that Merrill disagreed to get involved, Eugene's death would force the involvement down upon him. I'm assuming Merrill went there to finalize his membership with the board." Mimi surprises Bradley with this comment.

"Why didn't he put *you* down as the primary beneficiary?" Bradley wonders.

Mimi defends, "I don't want any part of Eugene and Tony's legacy. I didn't want my son to have any part in it either."

Now Bradley's curious, "But why did Eugene want him involved so badly?"

"Because of what he knows. Eugene wanted Merrill to help them develop medicinal defense tactics. Medical warfare." Mimi certainly knows how to captivate her audience, but Bradley already knows where this part's going.

Bradley thinks out loud, "So Merrill designed the programs for the pods?"

Mimi interjects, "Pods? What pods?"

Bradley lays it down, "I'm sorry to say, Miss Broussard, but the cause of your son's death was not from a stray bullet. I found several burn marks inside his body. They led from the bullet's entry point all the way to his heart, suggesting that multiple discharges of electricity passed through his right atrium until effectively reaching his heart and shutting it down."

Mimi's lost. "How's that even possible?"

"When I worked on the body of the shooter, I found five individual pods implanted in his brain. These pods were made up of thousands of microscopic robots all attached to each other. Except for the board members, every body I've worked on that's been directly involved with this shooting spree, has had these pods implanted somewhere in their bodies." Bradley is finally getting comfortable divulging his secret.

"What are these pods for?" Mimi wonders.

It's Bradley's time to inform, "Like you said, medical warfare. These bugs can be programmed to anywhere in the body and networked to attach to nerve receptors. They give off small electrical shocks to stun these receptors and inhibit bodily function. In Merrill's case, when the bullet hit him it shattered on impact and released billions of these robots. It probably only took a matter of minutes for the bugs to clump together and make it seem like Merrill then died from his wound."

Mimi responds, "I can't believe it."

"I'm sorry, Miss Broussard. I wish it wasn't true, but that's why I'm here. This massacre was not a coincidence. Someone was to gain from Magnus being torn apart. Who? What do you know about the five subsidiaries to Magnus? Starting with Walter Truax."

Mimi continues, "I told you. I didn't want anything to do with Eugene and Tony's legacy. I didn't want Merrill to have anything to do with it either. But that's all gone. It doesn't matter now. There's nothing you can do about it anyways."

Bradley pleads, "Please. I have to know."

"It appears you know a lot already," is Mimi's response.

Bradley wavers before asking, "How can I stop them?"

"You can't."

A moment of silence ensues before Mimi asks, "Would you care for more tea?"

Oddly enough, Bradley passes on the refill.

"Suit yourself." Mimi stands and walks back over to the kettle. As Mimi is refilling her cup, the doorbell suddenly rings.

Both Mimi and Bradley turn and look toward the front door wondering about the unknown and unexpected visitor.

To Bradley's dismay however, Mimi responds, "Ah. I was expecting company. That's the reason I happen to be here today. You were fortunate to come on a good day."

Mimi sets her teacup down on the stove and goes off to answer the door. Now Bradley is officially freaked out.

Mimi returns with unwelcome company. She leads with the comment, "Well, I guess there's no need for introductions."

Mimi enters the kitchen followed by Dr. Walter Truax and his entourage, his entourage being Generals Dobbs and Taylor.

Bradley quickly jumps up from his barstool and backs away.

Dr. Truax reassures him, "Relax, Dr. Simpson. We're only here to gain an understanding."

Bradley still recoils, "Yeah? An understanding of what?"

Dr. Truax takes a couple of small steps toward Bradley as he speaks, "Of just whose side you're on? I thought you knew what you were getting yourself into?"

Mimi sneaks in the suggestion, "Bradley, there's no need to uncover anything. They're not the bad guys. They're trying to help us. Help cure us."

Bradley asks with concern, "Mimi? Are you all right?"

"Never better." She replies.

Bradley tries reconfirming, "I told you what they're trying to do. They want to manipulate people."

Mimi, or something else, has already made up her mind. "Manipulate is such a harsh word. They're simply trying to formulate a procedure. One that we all must adhere to."

Walter suddenly interrupts, "Which reminds me, Mimi. Your part in this procedure has officially come to an end."

Mimi turns and looks at Walter. She speaks cautiously, "What are you saying?"

Walter admits his intent, "Since Merrill left you as the beneficiary on his will, in the event of your death, the inheritance will pass back to the corporation."

Bradley cuts Walter short to confer with Mimi, "What? But you said you weren't the primary beneficiary?"

Dr. Truax corrects, "She creates many a great fabrications, Dr. Simpson. The corporation as you already know, Miss Broussard, is controlled by the FDA and the American Medical Association. In other words: Us. You've fulfilled your part quite accurately, and for that I thank you."

Mimi beseeches Walter, "But I don't want the inheritance. Take it."

"I can't." Walter exclaims. "I'm sorry, Mimi."

"No, wait!" Mimi raises her arms in defense.

General Dobbs suddenly draws his sidearm and fires. The bullet strikes Mimi right between the eyes. Mimi Broussard's body falls hard to the floor.

Bradley can't hold back his reaction, "No! You son of a bitch!" Bradley runs toward Walter and the two Generals in hopes of breaking through their line and escaping out the front door.

General Dobbs prepares to fire but Walter stops him. "No. We need him alive."

Bradley runs full speed into their defense line but struggles to get by his three attackers. They pull and grab at Bradley attempting to subdue him. Finally, General Dobbs decides to take the butt of his gun and bash Bradley on the back of the neck. Bradley's body collapses but he isn't knocked out.

The two Generals grab a hold of Bradley and carry him over to a nearby armchair. Bradley's limp body slinks down into the chair and his shoulders slump while his head sways back and forth trying to recover from the blow.

Walter is now free to speak. "As you can see, Dr. Simpson, your dedication to truth and justice is pointless. You haven't even a vague comprehension of how deep we've infiltrated the system. The complexity of our prescription network can never be undone, and anyone that stands in our way will become a part of that system. So, I formally welcome you, Dr. Simpson."

Walter takes a syringe from his jacket pocket and injects its contents into Bradley's right median vein. Bradley's defenseless state offers no resistance.

"Help him up." Dr. Truax commands.

Dobbs and Taylor each take Bradley under the arms and lift him out of the chair.

Walter concludes, "It's time to go."

Walter makes for the front door while the Generals drag their wounded prey behind him.

The four men exit the estate and make their way through the yard toward the front gate. Since Bradley parked his SUV right in front of the gate, no other vehicles could get by him. A large, black, Chevy Suburban with tinted windows is parked beside the Mercedes. They must've totaled the luxury sedan.

Just as the men pass through the gate, a charcoal colored Crown Victoria suddenly emerges from the woods and comes to a stop. To Bradley's half-conscious delight, Detective Paige Dunbar steps out of her vehicle and stands alert behind the open car door.

"Police. What seems to be the problem here?"

Walter answers, "No problem, Detective."

Detective Dunbar recognizes Bradley's limp body resting in the hands of the two Generals. She asks, "Bradley? Are you all right? What's going on?"

Bradley's concussion type symptoms cause him to muffle his response. "Help me."

The detective struggles to hear. "What did he say?"

"Nothing. We're taking this man in for questioning." General Dobbs responds.

The men start to open the doors of the truck when Bradley re-iterates with a little more force, "Help me!"

Detective Paige Dunbar quickly draws her sidearm and takes aim. "Freeze!"

Both Generals drop Bradley's arms and allow him to fall to the ground. They draw their pistols in defense. Walter quickly opens the driver door of the Suburban and gets behind the wheel.

General Dobbs squeezes off the first shot. Detective Dunbar takes guard behind the driver door and uses the space between her door and the car frame to open fire. The General's shot misses high, but Paige's shot hits Dobbs' left center mass and passes through his ribs. He bellies over and uses his left hand to apply pressure to his side.

General Taylor attempts to open the back passenger door while at the same time trying to engage the detective. General Taylor's shots are all over the place. Another well-placed bullet from Paige's gun enters General Taylor's left shoulder. The bullet exits clean with no collateral in the background, but the impact spins Taylor's body around and he collides into General Dobbs. Dobbs is knocked back to the ground while Taylor regains his balance and enters the vehicle.

Dr. Truax impatiently shouts, "Let's go! Let's go!"

Walter throws the truck in reverse before General Taylor can even close the door. They leave General Dobbs lying in the dirt.

Detective Dunbar has to jump left and out of the way of the Suburban as it comes crashing back into the driver's side of Paige's Ford. The collision rips off both Paige's driver's side door and the Suburban's back passenger door.

General Taylor continues firing as they drive off. Paige rolls to a stop and fires another shot into the truck, but to no avail. The Suburban disappears down the wooded driveway.

Paige comes to her feet and focuses her attention back on the injured Dobbs and weary Dr. Simpson.

General Dobbs slowly manages to stand. The whole side of his O.D. Greens is soaked dark-maroon from the blood.

Detective Dunbar reinstates policy, "Freeze! Don't move. You're under arrest, General."

As Detective Dunbar vigilantly approaches the hunched General, Dobbs suddenly pulls his handgun out from behind his back. They both get their shots off, but Paige already had the upper hand. A small trail of dirt kicks up as the General's shot misses low while Paige's shot strikes the General dead in the chest. His body pushes backwards before falling to the ground. General William R. Dobbs is dead. (Victory!)

Detective Paige Dunbar runs over to our wounded hero. By now, Bradley is able to sit up. He tries to catch his breath and suppress the nausea while regaining his composure from a pounding headache.

Paige asks, "Are you OK?"

Bradley's response is weak, "Yeah. I think so. They injected me with something."

Paige helps Bradley to his feet. He commends her while staring down at the General's body, "You're a hell of a shot, Detective. You remind me of my wife."

Paige enlightens him, "She's the one that told me where to find you."

Bradley cracks a smile on his face before replying, "My heroes."

CHAPTER 10

IMPOUNDED

Dr. Simpson and Detective Dunbar drive back into town in Paige's Crown Victoria. Paige was worried about Bradley driving himself home and possibly blacking out on the road from the trauma to his head. She looks over at Bradley and begins to see him in a whole new light. Admiring his strength and determination, their entwined pathways are constructing a camaraderie that'll eventually prove to be very useful.

"We should get you to the hospital. You have no idea what that injection might do to you." Paige suggests. Her black hair flaps in the wind due to the missing driver's side door. Both she and Bradley have to raise their voices in order to speak over the sound of the wind whipping through the vehicle. Paige wears her seatbelt, of course.

"No. I'm a sitting duck at the hospital. Take me home." Bradley responds. He adds, "By the way, when did you talk to my wife?"

The detective answers, "This morning. I stopped by to see if you found any more leads. She said you had gone up the foothills to the Broussard estate." Paige then adds, "What the hell were you up there chasing anyways?"

"Leads." Bradley responds. "One of the bystanders was related to Magnus's CEO. I needed to know why they were both at the diner that day." Bradley's tone of speech and lazy posture still show the signs of his fatigue.

"And what did you find out?" Paige wonders.

"Merrill met with the board members because apparently he was a partner." Bradley surprises Paige with the info.

"Merrill? As in Merrill Broussard?" She asks.

Bradley turns in curiosity, "Yeah. Why?"

"Our Captain is holding a benefit golf outing in his memory." Paige updates Bradley of the police department's involvement, but not necessarily in connection to the massacre. The detective remains curious, "What else did you find out?"

The still woozy Bradley shifts his weight and rubs his temples before replying, "It was weird. Mimi said that Merrill was adopted, but his DNA shares a match with Eugene. Other than that, not much. Walter shot Mimi before she could tell me any more." Bradley uncomfortably shifts his weight again while continuing to rub his forehead. Our hero slowly tries to regain his strength.

Paige reacts, "Mimi Broussard, the founder of the Outreach Program? Truax shot her?" Mimi had started the Outreach Program in 2004 in conjunction with the city council and local law enforcement in an attempt to beautify the city streets by offering shelter, clothing, even community service for those hardest hit by the economic downturn. Detective Dunbar is only aware of the program because of the charity drives that different city departments hold for the needy. And even though the project didn't clean the streets entirely, the free labor force did enrage city workers after dozens were laid off to increase the annual budget for more appropriate expenses.

Bradley eventually corrects himself, "No actually, General Dobbs shot her. But Truax gave the order."

"Damn it, Bradley!" Paige suddenly reacts, "Why didn't you tell me there was another body in the house? I have to get you to the station."

Bradley doesn't understand, "Why?"

Paige is somewhat overwhelmed at Bradley's lack of intuition. "Because I called in our little altercation in the mountains. I informed dispatch that there was one male victim outside the estate and that I was taking you in for medical treatment. Now there is one unaccounted body, your vehicle is still at the scene, and your fingerprints are probably all over the house. I know you took a shot to the head, but you need to wake up and smell the coffee. They're going to think you're a suspect now."

Bradley's response, "Oh shit."

"Yeah, oh shit."

A three-door, charcoal gray sedan pulls into the police station. Detective Dunbar unbuckles her seatbelt and simply steps out of her vehicle. Bradley has to open his door first.

The local precinct isn't exactly megalithic, but it's a substantial enough complex to claim a good portion of the city block. The east lot mainly provides parking for cruisers and SWAT vans, but there are enough spaces to accommodate some visitors. A blacked out, chain link fence stands in the background guarding what constitutes the police impound. Only authorized personnel are permitted.

The structure itself raises four stories and thick, vertical, concrete buttresses accent the front. Tinted, energy efficient windows fill the space between the parapets.

Detective Dunbar and Dr. Simpson ascend the steps to the station's main entrance. Just inside the door, an authority figure waits to confront the tag team duo.

Captain Thomas Garrett, a twenty-five year veteran to the police force, opens with the commentary, "Good work, Detective. Were you injured?"

Paige responds, "No, Captain. We're fine."

"We're?" Captain Garrett offers Bradley a look of distain.

The detective conveys her professional courtesy, "Sorry, Captain. This is Dr. Bradley Simpson." Paige then turns to the good doctor, "Bradley, this is Captain Thomas Garrett."

Bradley reaches his hand out for a proper introduction, but the Captain is strangely intermissive, "That'll do, Detective. Thank you for bringing him in. You're excused."

Detective Dunbar comes back, "But Captain, what about my report?"

Captain Garrett assures her, "Don't worry, Detective. You'll have plenty of time trying to explain why you shot a General in the United States Marine Corps. Until then, I just have to ask him a couple of questions. Dr. Simpson, if you would follow me?" And just as cold shouldered as ever, Captain Garrett turns and heads down the precinct's central corridor toward one of the interrogation rooms.

Bradley looks at Paige with a confused sense of apprehension as he slowly follows the Captain. Paige gives Bradley the same look of confusion before she whispers. "Go ahead. It'll be all right." Paige remains near the entrance lobby and watches Bradley trail off before she makes her way over to her favorite station: the coffee bar. A few pumps from the carafe and the nasty, hackneyed liquid helps bring the detective back to square.

Meanwhile, Captain Garrett reaches the end of the corridor and opens the door to a small, off-white room with two chairs and a lone wooden desk and waits on Bradley's reluctance. Bradley moseys his way into the interrogation room and the Captain closes the door behind him.

The interrogation room doesn't come equipped with the prototypical one-way observation window nor are their any microphones or audio recording devices present. Bradley fears this encounter will not pass satisfactorily.

The Captain starts things off with a simple order, "Have a seat, Doctor." He motions for Bradley to take the chair on the left side of the desk whereas he pulls his out from the corresponding right. Both men have a seat, for the examination process is now under way. Oddly deprived though, Bradley notices the Captain has no files or paperwork on hand as strategic prowess. Captain Garrett appears to be winging it as he goes.

Again, the Captain opens with the commentary, "You've had quite the busy day. Haven't you, Dr. Simpson?"

"It's definitely been more than I expected." Bradley responds.

"What brought you to the foothills to begin with? Even as a PhD, I doubt you were up there house hunting." Captain Garrett asks.

Bradley doesn't hesitate with his explanation, "I was following a lead on one of the victims I autopsied from The Avenue massacre."

"Following leads?" Captain Garrett interrupts, "That's a job for the authorities. You're a medical examiner."

Bradley can tell there's no toying with the Captain. He's been around too many blocks. "I know. I didn't mean to impose, but I needed to know why certain board members had family present."

Captain Garrett drops a bomb on Bradley's ignorance. "Like Eugene's son, Merrill?"

"His son?" Bradley wonders. "Mimi said they weren't related."

Captain Garrett leans into the table before speaking, "Mimi took custody of Merrill when Eugene gave him up for adoption. When Eugene's wife, Tabitha, became pregnant, Eugene wasn't exactly thrilled. And then mysteriously, she disappeared two weeks after his birth. I don't suppose you figured out why?"

"No." Bradley replies.

"I figured as much." The Captain doesn't seem to appreciate Bradley's newfound knowledge.

But Bradley sneaks in the question otherwise, "But why would Mimi lie to me?"

Though he's losing his patience, the Captain responds. "Maybe because she didn't know you well enough to trust you with the truth. The Broussard family always kept to themselves. I know because Merrill would donate money to help our various departments, but never once did he show up in person. We always received the money in the form of a cashier's check."

"So then Merrill *was* to be a partner?" Bradley asks.

Abandoning patience, Captain Garrett slams his hands down on the table before suddenly standing up. "You know what? Will you excuse me, Doctor? I'll be right back." Captain Garrett glares at Bradley before turning and exiting the room.

Bradley's state of surprise from the Captain's sudden irrational reaction seems to distort his thoughts. Assumingly from the trauma to his head, Bradley tries to shake off his metaphysical cobwebs and regain focus. As though he stood up too fast and all the blood rushed to his head, Bradley takes deep breaths till his disorientation subsides.

While Bradley attempts to maintain his composure, the door to the interrogation room slowly reopens. However, it is not the Captain that enters.

Chief Inspector Dempsey is who crosses the threshold. The inspector walks over to Bradley but doesn't take the seat. Instead, he offers a very suspicious warning. Inspector Dempsey speaks quickly and with a hint of nervous hesitation. "Dr. Simpson? Do you remember me?"

"Yes." Bradley responds. "You're Chief Inspector Dempsey. You were the one that originally asked me to identify the three bystanders."

Inspector Dempsey continues, "And what did you find out?"

Bradley still has trouble focusing. He makes little eye contact with the inspector as he speaks, trying to withstand the nausea and loss of equilibrium. "Merrill was electrocuted, Saria was asphyxiated, and Terra suffered a massive heart attack."

Inspector Dempsey reacts, "God damn it! I knew it!"

Bradley suddenly looks up and realizes the anguish on the inspector's face. "What?"

Inspector Dempsey helps to thicken the plot. "Merrill was like a son to me. Mimi and I were dating when she decided to adopt him. She knew the kind of man that Eugene was and didn't want Merrill anywhere near him. Merrill went to The Avenue that day to forfeit his shares, not to become a member. The reason Merrill anonymously donated so much money to our different departments was because he was trying to buy us off to intervene on the company's corruption. Ever since Neurolex hit the market, he tried desperately to blow the whistle on Magnus. Once the corporation found out that Merrill designated Mimi as his beneficiary, he basically signed his own death warrant. Her's as well."

Inspector Dempsey pauses and goes back to the door to ensure the coast is still clear. He returns and continues educating Bradley. "You have to get out of here now, Dr. Simpson. I contacted your wife. She should be here in a couple of minutes."

Bradley responds confused, "What about Captain Garrett?"

Inspector Dempsey cuts Bradley short, "Captain Garrett is not a friend to you. He met with Dr. Truax of N.E.T.I. Pharmaceuticals about two weeks ago and ever since he returned, he hasn't been the same. He's experiencing symptoms similar to what you were experiencing when I entered the room. You have no idea the effects of what they put into you. They tried for years infecting Merrill, but his job at the Department of Defense required him to pass through a static chamber everyday. Truax has spent the last five years redeveloping a way for the bugs to withstand circuitry overload. If the Captain isn't placing you under arrest, he has no right to detain you. That's where he went. He's contacting Truax as we speak. Get out of here now!" And just like that, Chief Inspector Dempsey turns to exit the room. He opens the door.

Bradley stops the inspector, pleading, "But wait! How am I supposed to stop them?"

The inspector cuts him off again, "I have to go. Just get out of here." Inspector Dempsey quickly leaves the room while closing the door on his way out.

Not a minute later, Captain Garrett returns to his interrogation. "Sorry about that, Doctor. You'll be pleased to know that your vehicle is being taken to impound. So you can leave just as soon as it arrives."

To the Captain's surprise, Bradley stands up confidently exclaiming, "No, I think I'll leave now."

Captain Garrett remains standing between Bradley and the exit. "No. Take your seat, Doctor. I'm not done with my examination."

"Am I under arrest?" Bradley asks.

The Captain cannot lie his way out of this question. "No."

"Well then I'm out of here." Bradley attempts to walk passed Captain Garret, but the Captain grabs a hold of his arm on the way by.

"Spoken like a true criminal." Captain Garrett exclaims. "Or at least like someone recently educated on the inner-workings of our impartial system. I'll warn you, Dr. Simpson, I don't believe in the neutrality of the law. I always get my man."

For some reason, Bradley decides to resurface his ostentatious side with the comment, "How romantic. If you would like, I could use my phone call to contact my lawyer. Update him on the police brutality that takes place here at this precinct." Bradley stares down at the Captain's kung fu grip around his arm.

Captain Garrett tightens his grip and pulls Bradley in close. "Would you like me to show you police brutality?"

Just then, the door to the interrogation room suddenly opens. An officer enters and is somewhat shocked at what he sees. He asks, "Is everything all right, Captain?"

Captain Garrett releases Bradley's arm and responds, "Fine, fine, Officer. What can I do for you?"

"Dr. Simpson has a visitor. His wife is here to pick him up"

"How romantic." replies Captain Garrett.

Bradley steps in to take advantage of the opportunity. "Well, as fun as this was, Captain Garrett, I have to go now. After you, Officer."

Bradley walks passed the Captain, waits for the officer to turn and lead the way, and then exits the room. Captain Garrett remains standing there watching as his prey narrowly slips out the door.

Bradley and the officer make their way down the central corridor to the main lobby where Audrey waits to spring her husband. Bradley acknowledges her in his own typical fashion, "Hey, honey! How's it going?"

Audrey's response, "How in the hell do you think its going? Just go get in the car. We'll talk about this on the way home." Bradley's smile fades and he lowers his head while continuing passed Audrey and out the main entrance.

Detective Dunbar, the cop behind the receiving desk, and the officer who retrieved Bradley, cover their mouths in hopes of hiding their laughter. Audrey's iron will impresses even the most hardened of individuals.

Audrey turns to the officer behind the reception desk. "Is there anything that I have to sign, or...?"

The officer assures her, "Nope. You're free to go. Enjoy."

"Yeah. Thanks." Audrey performs an about-face with dignifying posture and exits the police station after her husband.

With Captain Garrett looming in the background, observing Audrey as she leaves, he realizes that Bradley's ride home should prove just as interesting as the interrogation room. He wouldn't want to mess with Audrey either.

Audrey walks up to her white, four-door BMW, where Bradley waits as he has already taken the passenger seat. Audrey enters the vehicle and begins reprimanding without a moments hesitation. She starts the car, buckles up, and drives off as she speaks. "Well, I hope you're happy. I had to cut my seminar short so that I could come bail your ass out of prison. I feel like I'm picking up Jacob from detention."

"I'm sorry. Thank you." defines our fearless leader.

"Don't thank me." Audrey responds. "Don't you think you're biting off a little more than you can chew? You continue to involve yourself and your family, but who appointed you to head up this investigation? Your job is to identify the bodies and determine a cause of death, nothing more."

Bradley buds in, "Yeah, and I did that, just to find the most technologically advanced form of mechanical microbiology that I've ever seen."

Audrey continues, "You found a black spec leaking out of a murderer's skull. Now you're pursuing this self-appointed conspiracy theory motive and doing nothing but implementing your own guilt. You're leaving a trail of involvement. It doesn't seem justifying. It seems self-incriminating. Who the hell was this guy anyways?"

"What guy?" Again, Bradley misses the punch line.

"What guy?" Audrey exclaims. "The shooter at The Avenue, genius. The one whose autopsy started this whole thing."

"I don't know. I just collected the physical data. I sent all the information over to Phil for identification." Too bad for Bradley all of his supporting witnesses are dropping like flies.

"Which reminds me, Dr. Pascoli called. He wanted to know why you haven't been showing up to work." Audrey informs.

Dr. Marco Pascoli is the superintendent of St. John's Medical Center. Bradley's boss.

CHAPTER 11

BACK FROM THE GRAVE

It's the next morning. Bradley wakens from his nightly slumber looking forward to another day of investigation, dodging bullets and assassination attempts, getting arrested, and most importantly, leaving a trail of self-incriminating evidence. He descends the stairwell wearing his favorite grayish beige robe accented with squares of various sizes in alternating shades of brown.

Bradley meets Jacob in the living room. Jacob lies in his usual belly down position on the carpet watching television.

"Morning, Jakey", offers Bradley.

"Morning, Dad", he responds. "How was prison?" As like any child might, Jacob says the darnedest things.

Bradley doesn't have to put much thought into his response, "Short and sweet."

"Were you molested?" Jacob effectively grasps his father's attention with this comment however.

"What?"

Jacob enlightens him, "Well, I hear prisons are just large institutions of man-love."

Though dumbfounded, Bradley exerts the obvious, "You watch entirely too much television."

"I know," says Jacob. "Which reminds me, they mentioned your name on T.V."

Bradley is slowly becoming concerned over his son's exemplary fondness of informative degradation. "Who mentioned my name?"

"Abra Malone from Live Action News." While Bradley's paranoia continues growing, Jacob seems totally at peace with the current events.

"When was this?" Bradley asks his son.

"This morning's broadcast. Something about a shooting, two dead bodies, your truck being impounded, and how you were brought in for questioning but then later released." Jacob could easily aspire to be the channel-surfing champion of the world. He grants each station its due glimpse of two to three second intervals before moving on. Though in this case, he made an exception.

"Are you serious?" As if Bradley's paranoia wasn't great enough.

"Yep." Jacob responds. "Like you said, I watch entirely too much television."

"Well, why don't you watch your cartoons or something?" says Bradley.

"Ah, they're for kids." Jacob informs his father.

"How silly of me." Bradley decides to continue through the living room into the kitchen as Jacob has successfully provided the perfect morning buzz kill.

Audrey, sporting her own favorite red satin robe, sits at the kitchen table drinking coffee and reading the newspaper. She welcomes her hubby as always, "Good morning, sleepyhead."

Bradley reciprocates, "Good morning, dearest."

The lovebirds exchange their initial peck on the lips and then Bradley heads toward the coffee pot.

Audrey speaks without divesting her gaze from the paper. "Did Jacob tell you the good news?"

"What? That yesterday's encounter is all over the television?"

"And the paper."

"Yeah, he gave me the short and skinny." Bradley tries to lose himself in the milky swirl of the coffee creamer as it blends with the dark roast.

"So, what are you going to do?" Audrey's concern is conflicted by her resolve.

But Bradley realizes conventional wisdom, "I'm going to work."

Audrey elates, "Good boy." Bradley turns and stares at her with a hint of insult by Audrey's childish martinet demeanor. She soon concedes, "Sorry."

"No, you're right," accepts Bradley. "My job is at the hospital. Not in the foothills chasing around some conspiracy theory and then getting blamed for it all. Sometimes it's better not to get involved." Our hero seems to be questioning his potential.

"Thank you." While Audrey for the first time, actually seems passive aggressive. "Whenever you're ready then." She digresses.

As to anyone's surprise, Bradley misses the punch line, "Ready for what?"

"To get your car out of impound."

Oh yeah. You can't very well go to work without a means of getting there.

The white, four-door Beamer returns to the police station, but this time however, Bradley isn't met with hostility. He simply hops out of the car, offers his name to the post guard, signs some paperwork, and signals Audrey with thumbs up.

Though Audrey seems a little bent out of shape over her spouse's criminality, she still upholds her devotion by waiting for the blacked out fence to open and for Bradley to repossess his vehicle assuring that he successfully drives out of harm's way. Eventually, they both go their separate ways, duty calls.

Dr. Simpson graciously slides into his land of bread and butter. His usual parking spot is already occupied, so Bradley opts for its neighbor. Bradley exits his vehicle and stares at the intruding silver Dodge Dart with consternation.

Using the same entrance as always, Dr. Simpson heads toward his office eager to catch up on the work that he's missed. Bradley opens the door that boldly demonstrates his name, depicts which department the door leads, and the physician assumingly in charge and enters.

Dr. Marco Pascoli awaits Bradley's arrival with the same eagerness that motivated Bradley to return to work. The hospital's superintendent rarely has time to visit staff members.

Bradley approaches his boss cautiously, "Dr. Pascoli. I heard you called. What can I do for you?"

Marco possesses a ploy of his own, "Dr. Simpson, welcome back. We were wondering when, or if, you would ever show up again."

Bradley tries to explain, "I'm sorry Superintendent. I was..."

Dr. Pascoli interrupts, shaking off Bradley's last premeditated thought.

"Yeah, yeah, yeah. Don't tell me. I already saw it over this morning's newscast. From now on, Dr. Miller will be taking over your responsibilities at this office. He has to examine the seven *other* bodies that have piled up in hopes of your return while you're preoccupied investigating the first seven. I was not aware that you were also a detective."

Bradley tries again, "But...?"

But Dr Pascoli doesn't allow the edge. "Dr. Simpson, you will be put on administrative leave, with pay, for a week's time. So whatever it is you're looking for? I suggest you find it and find it fast, so that you can go back to doing your job."

Bradley sets his intent in motion, "In point of fact, I returned to check on Phil's results from an autopsy I sent him."

Dr. Pascoli aptly responds, "Well, if that's what you have to do, then take care of it, and make sure you exit my premise promptly."

"Yes, Superintendent." Bradley turns to leave but Dr. Pascoli adds one final comment.

"Good luck, Doctor. I look forward to seeing your results."

Bradley exits the Medical Examiner's Office, closes the door behind him, and makes it halfway down the hospital corridor before he finally realizes, "Dr. Pascoli just gave me a week's paid vacation. He mentioned the seven *other* bodies. He told me to take care of whatever I had to do. And that he looks forward to seeing my results? Holy shit! He's on my side! He's actually encouraging my investigation of this case."

Bradley's newfound confidence causes him to disregard the vehicular evacuation and march straight for the Coroner's Office. After safely navigating the parking lot, he enters Phil's former edifice determined to find answers.

However, a sudden sense of apathy rushes over Bradley when he sees Valerie Dugan residing behind the reception desk. Her presence rekindles their last interaction, when Bradley witnessed his friend and colleague suffer from a mental breakdown just before being shot in the back and killed. Bradley slows his indomitable pace before engaging Valerie.

"Hey, Val." Dr. Simpson treads lightly.

Valerie looks up without her usual spunkiness. "Oh hey, Dr. Simpson." She responds typically, but now that easy-going manner of her tone is heavily weighed down from such a tragic upheaval of normalcy.

Bradley asks politely, "Would you mind if I looked at a file report from one of Phil's finalizations?"

Valerie concedes as always, "Not at all. Which file?"

Bradley didn't consider that part. "Um, I'm not exactly sure."

"Well, what's the name?"

"I don't know." Bradley isn't big on prerequisites.

Valerie however, still maintains part of her endearing quality. "With all do respect, Dr. Simpson, you're not exactly narrowing it down for me. Do you have *anything* on the person's identity?"

Bradley regains his apprehension. He told his wife he was done getting involved. Bradley speaks softly, "Well, he was the shooter in The Avenue massacre."

Valerie's eyes widen at Bradley's request. "Are you sure?"

"Yeah. Why?" Bradley doesn't understand.

"You'll see. Ask and you shall receive." Valerie rolls her office chair over to the filing cabinet, fingers through various documents, and pulls out an envelope from its resting place. She rolls back over to the window and extends the document to Bradley. "Prepare to have your socks knocked off."

Now Bradley is afraid. Similar to the promise he gave his wife this morning, Valerie is well aware that some things are better left alone, but our stubborn hero must know the truth. Bradley slowly opens the document like it was a Jack-in-the-Box and how some unforeseen force will ultimately jump out and bite him. Sure enough, Dr. Simpson reads the report and is suddenly hit with a ton of bricks. The good doctor can't hold back his reaction. "What! Are you shitting me?"

The identity of the shooter: Tony Vicelli.

Valerie understands Bradley's frustration, "Yep. That's what I said. Except I added the 'F' word."

Since Bradley isn't exactly primed in the tactics of conspiracy, he responds, "This can't be right."

"Oh, it's right."

Bradley removes his gaze from the file and focuses on Valerie. "I don't believe it. So he murdered his own executive board members?"

Valerie responds, "A dead man can't exactly murder anyone. Can he?"

Bradley gasps as he continues to come to grips with the gravity of this cover-up. "So he faked his own death?"

"Or so it would seem."

"Well, if Tony was supposedly the shooter, but he was already dead, then whose body did I actually perform the autopsy on?" Bradley's question appears to have crossed the line of Valerie's comfort zone. She suddenly looks down out of nervousness and stops the informative conveyance. "I'm sorry, Val." Bradley reassures, "It's all right. You don't have to tell me." Bradley releases a sigh of anxiety before running his fingers through his hair in search of relief. "I have to figure this out. If they're not stopped, who knows the type of power they'll have over people. I can't let that happen." Bradley hands Valerie back her file and turns to leave.

Valerie suddenly stands up and offers her concern, "Bradley! Be careful. I fear this massacre goes way too deep for our understanding and we're probably better off not knowing. They got to Phil. I don't want to see them get to you too."

Bradley knows Valerie is truly concerned now. She never uses his first name. But Bradley must remain confident. "They won't. I'll figure it out. I have to figure it out, for everyone's sake."

Bradley exits the Coroner's Office with an eerie feeling of déjà vu. Dr. Truax previously warned Bradley to keep his secret to himself for everyone's sake.

Bradley crosses the parking lot and finally decides to take the superintendent's advice. He gets in his vehicle and exits the premise promptly in order to continue investigating the bystander leads. Next on the list: Mumahd and Saria Zehata.

But first, Bradley must find a Wi-Fi hotspot before he can return home. Audrey checks their computer's history everyday and he's supposed to be done following leads.

CHAPTER 12

ADMINISTRATIVE LEAVE

Satieri Abdul Zehata was born in Bangalore, India. Satieri's father, Jahgdis, was a successful land contractor who approved American or European companies cost-effective lease permits to secure facilities at little cost to property tax and/or labor wages. Known in the negative format as sweat shopping, proceeds could then be distributed amongst partners as opposed to the workers or the country's economy for the purpose of mere exploitation without representation. After the cost inflation of whatever products these companies manufactured and exported, the unethical venue created gain of exponential value.

Satieri quickly grasped an understanding of market trend numerals, or alternatively understood as profit-over-cost ratios. Being that a lot of the remunerations were off the books, little to no standard of auditing was even applicable. Plus, a lack of government regulations doesn't help either.

Jahgdis's success not only infuriated locals by dilapidating much of Mysore's southern provinces, but it also enabled the financial freedom for Satieri to attend school at The Indian Institute of Science. Satieri simply pursued his education in medicine after his father almost died from a sinus infection during his sophomore year as an undergrad.

In the early nineteen seventies, a tragic accident at one of Jahgdis's facilities claimed the lives of one hundred and eighteen workers and caused Satieri to abandon his scientific roots and not just leave for America, but flee to America. Jahgdis and much of Satieri's family did not survive the people's insurrection.

Satieri Zehata established his first medical practice in Trenton, New Jersey where he still resides to this day. He would occasionally spend his nights doing scientific work at a classified location with partners whom a majority of their identities have been withheld from public access. Not the historical records, just certain availability.

The original application of fiber-optic technology was years in the making that required countless hours of research before the scientific community broke ground on development. Though some conspiracy theorists contribute the advancement to findings from the Roswell crash site, the ability to gather video feedback by wire took hard work and dedication that opened previously closed doors in the fields of medicine, reconnaissance, telecommunications, engineering, even search and rescue without crediting reverse-engineering to the technologies of little green men. The credit would be given where it should: to the laboratory and scientists responsible for real-world application.

However, Satieri was never formally recognized for any scientific invention because technically, he doesn't exist in the community.

Mumahd Omar Zehata was born in 1979 only a few years after Satieri exiled himself to America. A lab partner of Satieri's back in Bangalore followed the young scientist/doctor to America at his own request. Roma Arana became Roma Zehata to gain citizenship under Satieri's professional amnesty. Topped off with a Visa card, corporate tax breaks, and full medical coverage, the young couple's secure foundation found it plausible to commence a family.

Young Mumahd spent his eager childhood at study more often

than play. After skipping not only second and fifth grade, Mumahd graduated from high school as salutatorian by his junior year. His educational background and family reputation ushered Mumahd into the country's most accredited technical institutes where they actually competed for Mumahd's enrollment. And not just as an undergraduate, but grad school as well.

After obtaining his Physical Doctrine, Mumahd resplendently returned as an assistant to his father's practice with congenial aptitude. It took roughly five years of servitude before Mumahd disbanded and partnered with Satieri's former colleagues for the sake of apportioning their scientific and technological novelties, hence market value for the research and development aspect. Mumahd eventually agreed to an executive position being that his joint venture attracted Magnus Medical Distribution Corporation as the primary benefactor. Mumahd was held in high esteem for his ability to spot the next big thing.

Mumahd and Saria attended medical school together and apparently dated for years before they finally decided to tie the knot. It was a long-lasting, loving, and romantic relationship that rivals even the most inspiring high school sweetheart's stories.

After a grueling and extensive online search, our hero Dr./ Detective Simpson could only collect such information on his next target. Though the Zehata legacy appears to be a very troubling and traditional amalgamation, the tricky part for Bradley is how he's going to convince his wife that he must now travel to Trenton. With a week's paid vacation however, he could convince Audrey to visit her family in Philadelphia. It's just a stone's throw away.

Bradley pulls into his driveway being that he was sent home early for a whole week. The exultation of getting paid without working for the next seven days is quickly extinguished by the fear of responsible disclosure. He knows his wife will be upset with him. Like she said earlier, it's similar to dealing with Jacob after being sent to detention.

The Simpson home rests in a quiet, upscale middle-class neighborhood with decently sized three-story abodes, large front and back yards, a safe and welcoming atmosphere where children play outside, people walk their pets, and the ice cream truck frequents the area during the summer months. Bradley usually spends his weekends mowing the yard or doing chores and basic maintenance in or around the house. That is if he's not unexpectedly called into work. The Simpson family boasts a prideful domain.

Today though, Bradley's pride seems to be seeping out all over his unkempt lawn. With his head held low, Bradley reaches for the front doorknob and opens the entrance to his domain with a wavering sense of impending punishment. His spirit is somewhat lifted when he enters to a festive scene of family videogame combativeness.

Audrey sits on the couch while Jacob lies (where else) on the carpet. The sporadic tapping of buttons drowns out the serenity as they engage in one of Jacob's favorite first-person shooter games. Their inaccurate enhancement of the complex simulations cause them to pretty much fire in all directions and simply hope to hit something. For the most part though, it's cute, and therefore must force a smile upon our hero's face.

Remaining unnoticed, Bradley holds back by the entrance enjoying the moment while it lasts. As Bradley observes the battle unfold on the television set, he can't help but notice a distortion in his visual clarity. The picture becomes fuzzier with each passing moment. He attempts to rub his eyes for relief, but the dizziness spreads and Bradley can't seem to shake away the vertigo. Scanning over the living room, the good doctor appears to be losing his focus, depth perception, and equilibrium. A slight headache ensues followed by a strong feeling of nausea. Bradley sets the soft-sided briefcase down in the front foyer before pressing his fingers against his temples to try coping with the discomfort. His face winces in pain.

Only then does Audrey notice her hubby standing in the doorway. "Why hello, honey. I didn't see you standing there."

Jacob looks away from the TV to acknowledge his father's presence. "Oh hey, dad."

Both Audrey and Jacob observe Bradley pinching his temples in anxiety while consequently, both of their characters are taken down in the videogame because of the distraction.

Jacob looks back at the TV with general dismay and exclaims, "Oh man! I was on a streak." Jacob returns to the game ready for a second chance while Audrey maintains her attention on her suffering husband.

"Bradley? Are you OK?" she asks.

Bradley takes his hand away from his forehead and opens his eyes. To his delight, the lightheadedness slowly subsides and he can see straight again. Somewhat concerned but not overly excited, Bradley responds, "Yeah, I'm fine. I think the blood just rushed to my head a little too fast when I stood up." Bradley motions to the briefcase he recently set down. Bradley quickly changes the subject, "So, who's winning?"

Since Audrey loves toying with her son, she quickly exclaims, "I am." She knows Jacob is highly competitive and will fire back in defense.

Jacob responds, "Yeah, if you call cheating winning." And so it begins.

Audrey returns with the comment, "I'm not cheating. Don't be mad because I'm a General and you're just a Sergeant."

Jacob's comeback, "I'm the Commander and Chief."

Bradley corrects his son's youthful ignorance, "I think its Commander-in-Chief."

Jacob says, "Oh. Well either way, she's still cheating."

"I am not!" Audrey doesn't budge.

Bradley knows their spirited arguments can last for minutes, even hours, so he picks up his briefcase and continues through the living room offering one last piece of advice, "Remember to play nice, you two."

With his back turned, Bradley is given a simultaneous response, "We will."

Bradley makes his way over to a series of coat hooks arranged near the kitchen door and sheds his effects. His next plan lies within the study to search online for possible travel arrangements to Philly, but Audrey finally enters the kitchen and blocks his escape.

"You're home early. How'd it go?" she asks.

Bradley slumps his brow slightly, "It could've been better."

"Were you fired?" Audrey shows general concern by her tone.

"No. Administrative leave." Bradley replies.

Audrey asks, "What's administrative leave mean?"

This is the part where Bradley is unsure of his wife's reaction. "They're paying me not to show up for work."

"For how long?" Audrey wonders.

"A week." Bradley holds his breath.

Audrey's reaction, "Really? That's pretty cool. I mean not for your reputation, but at least you're getting paid."

Bradley looks up at his wife and cracks his usual smile of juvenile reprieve. "Yeah, I wasn't too upset about a free vacation."

Unknowingly, Audrey sets herself up with the next question, "So, what are you going to do with your newfound freedom?"

Bradley has to remember to dance around the subject. Acting too verbose might give away his premeditation. "Oh, I don't know. I thought about maybe visiting Marge and Roger. Jacob hasn't seen them since what, last summer?"

"Really? You never want to visit my parents." Audrey isn't wrong with her assessment. Roger is a psychiatrist who is convinced that Bradley suffers from depression because he works with dead people all day long. Roger personally believes that Bradley represses his emotions as to not worry or subject the innocence of his daughter and grandson to his sociopathic tendencies. Their conversations are quite entertaining and inevitably futile. So obviously, why would Bradley wish to subject himself to such scrutiny? In all reality, Bradley doesn't wish to spend much time with him at all.

Bradley's superficial response, "I thought it would be nice to just get away for a couple of days."

Audrey is somewhat suspicious of his sincerity, but she has to admit, "Yeah, I guess it could be fun to drive down for a couple of days. But not today."

"No? Why not?" Bradley almost slips up when he doesn't take into account Audrey's sense of responsibility.

She informs him, "Because this house is a mess, we're not even packed yet, and you have to mow the lawn first."

All Bradley can say is, "Oh. OK."

CHAPTER 13

PHILADELPHIA BLUNDER (PART 1)

Bradley chooses his beige Mercedes to make the five hour drive down to Philadelphia. Audrey argued that her Beamer would get better gas mileage, but Bradley needed his ride for the freedom to pick up and leave whenever convenient. If they took Audrey's car, Bradley would have a terrible time explaining why he must take off momentarily and not bring his family with him. Plus, he convinced her that his SUV would be more comfortable now that the bumper is reaffixed. After he mowed the yard yesterday, Bradley took the truck into the shop to assure it was roadworthy.

Unfortunately, being that Bradley opted to take his once confiscated vehicle, it is unbeknownst to who or what may be tracking the family's excursion.

In the meantime, while the Simpson family is on the road, another breaking news report is currently being delivered back at home.

"This is Abra Malone for Live Action News reporting downtown from the city's Medical Center. The Neurological Engineering Technology Institute, also known as N.E.T.I. Pharmaceuticals, has just released plans for the distribution of their new compound, Equinox. N.E.T.I. Pharmaceuticals is one of the five, government financed organizations that formed out of the dissolution of the

Magnus Medical Distribution Corporation. The compound was actually developed at the self-named Equinox laboratories, but manufacturing and distribution will take place through N.E.T.I. Though the Chief of Operations for N.E.T.I. Pharmaceuticals, Dr. Walter Truax, was not available for comment, a spokesperson for the FDA assured that if taken correctly, little to no side effects of the drug was to be expected. Formerly known as Neurolex, the upgraded Equinox is a compound that'll be prescribed for individuals suffering from nervous disorders that include depression, dementia, and schizophrenia, and should hit pharmacy shelves within the month. A panel of experts did report such symptoms as mild to severe headache, nose bleeding, and slight disorientation. As for the distribution of the drug, it should be covered under most medical insurance policies and therefore should not increase premiums or deductibles. The other independent compounding companies have reportedly come online with similar psychoactive inhibitors for disorders ranging anywhere from indigestion to the atrophying of organs and skin cells. Though the compounds are not designed to prevent or replenish internal damage already sustained, the inhibitors should quell the pain of certain symptoms due to the response of nerve receptors, while additional compounds for the repair of such damages will come online in the following months. It appears that the collapse of the Magnus trademark has in fact, opened doors that'd been previously closed because of internal disparities. With solutions near to the future of medical treatment, many are actually rejoicing in the innovations soon to come. For this breaking news report, this is Abra Malone live from the city's Medical Center."

A freshly damaged, three-door black Suburban is parked in the lot of N.E.T.I Pharmaceuticals. Sitting in the comfort of his secure facility, high within the foothills, Dr. Truax watches the afternoon news report with extreme abhorrence. "A spokesperson from the FDA my ass! We own the god damn FDA! She is receiving inside information from someone. We have to find out who."

General Taylor, with his left shoulder in a sling, walks up behind Dr. Truax and sets a cup of coffee down on his desk.

Walter continues, "General, I think it's time for Miss Malone's impartiality to come to an end."

"Understood, Doctor." General Taylor retreats from Walter's office. He heads out on a new mission of operation.

Meanwhile, an operator that's monitoring a communications control panel turns in his chair toward Walter's office and beckons, "Dr. Truax? I think you better come see this."

Walter hates interruptions. So he responds with a sense of sullenness. "What is it?"

"One of our courier signals is on the move," replies the operator.

"What?" Curiously, the bad doctor removes his attention from the television and goes into the lab to investigate the disturbance. "Whose signal?" Walter asks.

The operator responds as any computer readout might, "SL3-17190."

A cunning smirk forms on Dr. Truax's face. "Huh, seventeen one-ninety. Where's he going?"

The operator punches some commands into the keyboard and answers, "He seems to be heading south. Towards Philadelphia."

"Ah, visiting an old friend," remarks Dr. Truax. He maintains directive over his operator, "You know what to do. Keep an eye on his movements." Walter then withdraws back to his office.

"Yes, Doctor." The institute's correspondents maintain as they should, timidly precise.

Dr. Simpson and his family finally arrive at their destination. Philadelphia in the summertime presents an engaging scenic comfort, but the city of brotherly love conceals such underlying dispositions that only the ordained can depict subtle vagrancies.

The beige Mercedes passes beyond the magnificent business district and cruises through the streets of boxed housing in observance of depleted economic augmentation before their evasion from trite exposes affluent substantiality. The Hilliard family resides contentedly apart from the harsh exposure to desperation. The gracious presentiment rivals only that of Bradley's kindred heritage. Accomplishment overcomes misfortune.

Roger and Marge Hilliard claim a grand occasion on the banks of the "Main Line." Roger's successful psychiatric practice coupled with Marge's lucrative career as a financial agent has combined into a silver-spoon fed paradise. Their mansion is located in the town of Haverford, where Audrey's college career started off just over the railroad tracks. The house is made of pinkish rose brick and decorative concrete inlay that's used as window trimming which highlight the various blooms of Marge's favorite flowers. Roger spends a majority of his free time reading within their enclosed back porch which overlooks the fairly small surround that mimics much of the neighborhood with crisp, clean-cut appeal only yards apart. (Relatively under-embellished.)

Audrey's return home reminds her of the lavish, only child upbringing that she lost interest in expecting as an adult. Though she and Bradley aren't exactly roughing it, Audrey is far from a gold-digger. She initially pursued a career in finance, but after hearing enough cloak and dagger regarding corporate corruption while witnessing certain company's atrocious neglect toward their employees, Audrey decided to follow a law degree in the defense of the little guy. Her online service, which adaptively blows the whistle on such divergences, has attracted friends as well as enemies.

The SUV pulls into the driveway and around to the back of the house next to Roger's favorite lounging area. As Bradley parks the vehicle in front of the garage, Roger removes his attention along with his glasses from the current novel he's reading, and stands to greet his daughter and grandson. Audrey and Jacob have already exited the vehicle and approach the patio.

Marge opens the sliding glass door of the house and walks out onto the back floor while Roger holds the patio entrance open for their visitors.

Roger begins with the greeting, "Hey! There's my big man. How've you been, Jake?" Roger holds out his hand and greets Jacob.

Jacob returns the handshake, "Not bad, grandpa. How've you been?"

"I try not to complain." Roger replies.

Jacob walks past his grandfather and into the lounge as Audrey follows close behind. "Hey, dad." She says upon entering.

"Hey, honey. How are things?" Roger turns a cheek as his daughter offers a cordial kiss that leaves him with a blush red imprint.

Audrey then answers, "Oh, you know me. I try not to complain either."

"That's my girl." Roger turns and lets the door shut behind him as Bradley has just exited the vehicle and slowly proceeds toward the lion's den.

Meanwhile, Jacob greets his grandmother. "Hey, grandma."

"Hey, Jakey," she says before asking, "Got a hug for your old grandma?"

Jacob leans in and allows Marge to squeeze the life out of him. "Oh! Look how big you're getting." Marge relieves Jacob from her death grip and moves on to her daughter, "There's my baby," maintaining verbal maternity.

"Hey, mom." Audrey is well accustomed to her mother's bear hugs, so she just inhales and rests her chin on Marge's shoulder while being constricted.

Both ladies sigh uncontrollably from the embrace. Marge sighs with jubilation while Audrey sighs from suffocation.

Marge unleashes her daughter just as the patio door opens and Bradley enters to a dead silence. Everyone turns to see this intruding person unconvincingly smiling at them and expecting to board the same welcome wagon. However, no such luck.

Marge replies, "Oh, hi Bradley."

"Marge! How've you been?" Bradley opens his arms and attempts to engage a hug, but before he can even take a step, Marge disruptively turns back to Audrey and Jacob.

"Why don't you two come inside? I'm sure you're tired from your trip." Marge interrupts and evades with precision. The three of them retreat into the house while the two boys have a chance to play outside.

Bradley extends his hand and voices the greeting, "Roger, it's always a pleasure."

Roger accepts Bradley's gesture and submits his handshake. "Likewise, Bradley. How's the mortician business?"

Bradley's facetious response, "Oh, you know. Some days are livelier than others."

Roger can only reply with strained animosity, "I don't doubt that."

Just then, Bradley realizes the origins of his ostentatious side: to repel the cynicism brought forth by his in-laws. Bradley thinks amiably to himself on how proud Roger would be of his subjective progress. (It takes two-of-a-kind to tango.)

Since Roger is well learned in the ways of slight, he casually moves through the tension. "Have a seat." Roger motions for Bradley to take the chair next to him and the end table that holds his reading glasses, a drink of water, and his recent hardback.

Bradley accepts, "Thank you. What are you reading?"

"Thomas Trimble," Roger replies. Thomas Trimble is well-known for his psychological thrillers that pit unsuspecting victims into complex and formidable obstacles that require personal loss so that the antagonist can exact vengeance against an undermining and unappreciative society. Almost like Edgar Allan Poe without the same intellectual pizzazz, or Saw movies without the same haphazard repetitiveness, Thomas Trimble does still hold his own.

"Yeah? Is it good?" Bradley attempts to avoid arbitration but can't really think of anything else to talk about.

"No." Roger replies, not exactly fond of small talk.

"That's too bad. His stories are usually a little spooky." Bradley is just buying himself time now. He knows he's never read any of the author's work.

"Speaking of spooky, what the hell is this I'm hearing about you in the news all the time?" A knot forms in Bradley's stomach as Roger cuts to the chase.

Bradley knows he can't divulge his secret to Roger or then he'll really think he's crazy. Bradley takes careful time not to rush his response, but Roger's blank stare insinuates that his patience is quite quickly wearing thin. Bradley is finally able to muster the pretext, "It was a very high-profile assassination. A lot of important people were killed and I'm solely responsible for explaining to the public why it happened. It puts a lot of pressure on one man."

"But being at the scene of two other murders afterwards? It seems like the media is suggesting that you're involved with more than just explanations. Care to enlighten me?" Roger is certainly not the man to trifle with. He knows his hardball.

Bradley can't help but initiate his frustrated defense mechanism, "It's called a scapegoat, Roger. The gravity of the massacre needs a fall guy to pin blame on so that the guilty parties can disappear scot-free. I happened to be at the scene of the two other murders following leads to try and clear my name."

"Following leads?" Roger replies. "So you're a detective now too? I thought you were just a mortician?"

It's on now! Bradley comes prepared for the battle of wits that he and Roger usually embody. "No, Roger. Actually, I'm a medical examiner. I perform autopsies on the recently deceased. You might've read about it at one point in one of your books."

Roger stands his ground. "Don't take that attitude with me, son."

Bradley responds, "Well, what do you expect? Every time I come over here, all you and Marge do is insult my intelligence."

Roger digs the proverbial knife a little deeper. "There has to be something there to insult."

"Thanks, that's much better. Your little head shrinking games don't work on me. You don't know me that well." Bradley counters.

"Actually, I know you better than you think. I know that when my own daughter calls me and says that you're coming, and she tells me it was your idea, something isn't exactly in place. What, did you miss me that much? Or is that what you're doing down here, following more leads?" Roger's good at leaving the ball in someone else's court with reverse psychology.

Bradley doesn't quit though. "No. I thought it would be nice for Jacob to see his grandparents before school started up again, or at least before they croaked."

"At the rate that you're going trying to clear your name, maybe *you* should spend more time with them. Before you beat us to the punch." Roger lays down the law with this comment.

Suddenly, Bradley stops. He lowers his eyes in contemplation and realizes that Roger might be right. Bradley has been so preoccupied chasing his theories that he hasn't spent much time with his family. Even before all of this started, Bradley always did prioritize his work first.

Roger acknowledges the fact that he struck a chord on Bradley's thought process and doused his belligerence. He reaches over and picks up his drinking glass, and while he stares into the clear abyss of his tap water, Roger proposes, "Let's go inside and get a drink. This isn't going to be strong enough."

Roger stands and waits for Bradley to concede. As he slides the back door open and Bradley stands to enter, Roger puts his hand on Bradley's shoulder and finally welcomes him into his home. "Marge should have dinner ready soon." The two absolved men proceed inside.

CHAPTER 14

THE ZEHATA FAMILY VALUE

Morning at the Hilliard's is anything but quiet, and sleeping in will not abide. Since Marge and Roger go to bed no later than eight thirty, they're up literally by the crack of dawn.

Last night's dinner consisted of smoked salmon fillets with cayenne pepper seasoning, water chestnuts and onion sprouts topped with white wine asparagus, and garlic vermicelli for the starch. Audrey and her mother indulged in the remnants of the white wine while Roger and Bradley polished off an eighteen year old bottle of scotch. They all had ice water as a subsequent chaser. Jacob had milk.

Though Roger only had two doubles before carting off to bed, Bradley consumed about four. Just to take the edge off.

The morning, along with Bradley's hangover, begins at a quarter after seven when the teapot whistles for arousal. Marge has already dressed, emptied the dishwasher and finished putting away the remnants of her gourmet meal, ran the vacuum cleaner, and planned the whole day's itinerary by the time the kettle sounds. Roger has also cleaned up, he's on his third cup of tea, and now peacefully rests in his usual spot reading the next chapter of thrill and mystery abound. Audrey has finished unpacking the SUV of their belongings, gotten dressed as well, and now enters the guestroom to kick Bradley out so that she can make the bed.

"Rise and shine, sleepyhead," is her introduction. Audrey usually doesn't have to go so far as to open the blinds or pull the comforter off of Bradley to wake him, but today she'll make an exception. She does both, starting with the blinds first, even though Bradley was already stirring.

"Oh, how could you?" is his blurred response.

"Sorry, my dear. But daylight's a wasting." Audrey sets a large suitcase on the bed next to her husband and begins to unpack various belongings while taking out a drawstring hamper for yesterday's dirty clothes.

As Bradley rolls out of bed, he claims, "Daylight hasn't even been up an hour yet, it can wait."

Audrey informs him, "Yes, but unfortunately, my parents can't. They have the whole day planned."

"Oh, joy and rapture." A weary Dr. Simpson staggers into the guest bathroom and closes the door.

Audrey in turn, arranges their suitcases and the laundry bag in a nearby corner and starts on the bed. She has already set aside an outfit for Jacob. He is her next victim.

Bradley eventually makes his way downstairs somewhat rejuvenated from the intoxicating nighttime escapade. Fully dressed, except for the towel around his neck to keep the water from his wet hair from absorbing into the new outfit, Bradley enters the kitchen to find Jacob at the table eating cereal and Audrey and Marge sipping tea while passing around their preferred sections of the newspaper. Bradley asks the obvious, "Audrey? Did you pack the hairdryer?"

"Yes." Audrey informs her husband. "It's in the side compartment of my suitcase."

Marge looks up at Bradley and starts things off as usual, "Well, look who it is. Have you recovered from your power hour yet?"

Bradley turns and looks back upstairs considering the hairdryer as a possible excuse to escape Marge. Instead, he decides that his hair is dry enough by now that it's not worth the hassle in comparison. He responds the best way he knows how, "It's too early to tell."

And of course, Marge always finds her angle, "Well, we don't have all day for you to sober up. We have a busy day ahead of us."

Bradley assumes her debasing demeanor is from living with a psychiatrist for so long, but since he broke ground on Roger's unyielding dissections yesterday, he figured he'd ask, "Where's Roger?"

Marge and Audrey both lift their heads to speak and Jacob simply points, but Marge happens to jump first. "Where do you think he is? On the porch reading one of his gory stories." Marge has always referred to Roger's choice in literature as gory stories, but Audrey thinks it's because he likes understanding how to profile the mind of a madman. A way for him to reassert job placement.

Audrey offers sensibility as she observes Bradley looking for a reason to escape the kitchen and Marge. "There's tea in the kettle if you'd like."

"Thank you, my dear. I would. Good morning by the way, in case I forgot." Bradley invokes manners as a lesson for Marge, but also because he forgot to offer his wife the gesture earlier.

"Oh, you never do, my dearest." Audrey certainly knows how to play along when it comes to the egocentricities of opulence.

"Hey, that's my line." Bradley shares a smile with his wife and relishes at the scowl on his mother-in-law's face. He pours a cup of tea and lightheartedly proceeds outdoors.

Roger is not much the conversationalist in the morning, as opposed to any other time of the day. When Bradley enters onto the porch, only a quick glance is what he receives. Bradley honors a nod and a word, "Morning." Still, no response is granted.

Since Bradley doesn't exactly exemplify equanimity, only of few moments of silence ensues before, "Lovely morning, isn't it?" and again, no rejoinder.

But Bradley can't help but persist, "Sleep well?" Roger releases a sigh of provocation. He shifts his weight to signify vocal retention, but Bradley just doesn't seem to catch the hint. "Marge says we have a busy day ahead of us. What did you feel like doing today?"

Finally, Roger breaks down. He turns toward Bradley and utters with impatient simplicity, "Whenever you're finished."

"Oh, sorry." Bradley withdraws to his solitude as Roger peacefully and quietly returns to his book. And that's when Bradley figures that Roger escapes to his porch for the same reason Bradley did, to escape Marge's insistent badgering.

They both sit there enjoying the serenity, the scenery, and the cool morning air when the patio door suddenly opens and the understanding shatters all to hell again.

"Hey, Roger? You about ready to get moving?" Marge asks.

Roger slams his book shut and exclaims, "Oh, for crying out loud." Roger looks back at Bradley, "Thanks." Roger stands up from his chair and makes his way inside.

Bradley tries to explain, "What? I didn't know. I was just trying to..."

Roger disappears inside the house while Marge stands there staring at Bradley. "What did you do?" She asks before disappearing inside as well.

Bradley remains in his chair stuck in a stupor. (You're damned if you do, you're damned if you don't.)

Assertive family value has congregated within the kitchen as a preemptive strike towards a well-laid plan. Among the day's agenda: shopping!

Roger, Jacob, and of course, Bradley stand opposed. However, Roger must follow where his wife deems worthy or face the wrath of a lady scorned, even though the silent treatment is not a bad result in his eyes.

Bradley stands firm that he'd rather head downtown for some sightseeing and that he could catch up with them at the restaurant where they plan to stop for lunch.

Unfortunately, Jacob requests, "Can I go with dad?" This is last thing that Bradley wanted. He'd hoped to travel to Trenton alone so that no one else would be put in harm's way, which is if harm were to be waiting.

After a few minutes of deliberation, Audrey agrees to let the boys go their own route while Roger is stuck with his ladies. He offers Bradley a slight glare as they exit the house and approach the driveway to load up.

Roger presses the button on his remote to open the garage before he shuts the back door. Roger just recently traded in his lease for a 2015 Lincoln Navigator. He has always been a Ford man, but a fellow make in Lincoln or Mercury is an acceptable alternative. For a gentle kick in the pants against Bradley's official shopping pardon, Roger asks him, "How's that foreign junk treating you?" referring to his Mercedes SUV.

Bradley can't help but implicate the joy of Roger's upcoming venture, "It makes for a very quiet ride."

Roger can only respond, "I hope it doesn't run out of gas backing down the driveway."

And of course, Bradley has to fire back, "It won't. It gets 33 miles-per-gallon on the highway. How about yours?"

Roger just climbs into his vehicle and slams the driver door shut, nipping their conversation in the bud.

"You boys be careful. Have fun." Audrey says as she opens the passenger door.

"Thanks mom, we will." Jacob replies.

"You too. We'll see you at lunch." Bradley devotes.

The two vehicles back out of the driveway and head their separate ways.

It only takes about thirty, forty minutes to drive to Trenton. But Bradley must make haste if he is to find Satieri's practice, figure out what Mumahd was doing at the diner, and drive back in time for lunch.

Jacob quickly noticed that they weren't going downtown to sightsee after they passed three exit signs depicting historical landmarks. Jacob apparently had a desire to view the Liberty Bell. "Where are we going?" was his request.

Bradley enlightens his son, "To visit a colleague. It'll only take a minute."

Jacob rolls his eyes knowing Bradley has again brought work along with him, even while on vacation.

Trenton shares the same colonial effect as Philly, just not quite as grand a skyline. The sturdy, well-built architecture resembles the endurance that a young nation presented as Washington famously crossed the Delaware to fortify the front in the Revolutionary War. His statue stands high above to symbolize an unyielding and uncompromising quality that demands equal treatment under the law. (Ironic?)

Our hero and his young sidekick must now stand *against* the same forces that be.

Bradley keeps his head on a swivel as they drive through town. Some of the small, local businesses are hard to determine by either the placards anchored into the concrete structures or the old wooden signs hanging by the entrances.

As the SUV stops at a light, Jacob has the good sense to ask, "What exactly are we looking for?"

Bradley confides, "His name is Zehata. He has his own medical practice. It said it was on Main."

"Yeah, it's right there." Bradley turns and looks out of the passenger window as Jacob points at an old, brick building bearing the sign: Satieri Zehata. Ear, Nose, and Throat Specialist.

"Oh, good boy." Bradley pulls into one of the few parking spaces set right on Main in front of the practice. Bradley and Jacob unbuckle themselves and go to exit the vehicle when Bradley requests, "Why don't you stay here. I'll only be a minute."

"Fine." Jacob closes his door and slouches back into the chair.

Bradley enters to small waiting room where an elderly couple occupies two of the dozen seats available. The receptionist quickly acknowledges Bradley's presence. "Hello? May I help you, sir?"

Bradley hoped to skip any formal introductions, but proceeds in the usual manner. "Yes. I was hoping to see Dr. Zehata."

"Do you have an appointment?" the receptionist asks.

"No. No I don't. I just needed to ask him a few questions." Bradley glances around the office space. Certificates and honorary awards cover the plaid wallpaper while photos of family members and other prominent businessmen dot the receptionist's office and waiting room end tables.

The receptionist continues, "What's the name?"

"Dr. Simpson."

"Well then Dr. Simpson, if you'll have a seat, the doctor will be with you shortly." The receptionist seems curious about Bradley's unscheduled conference call.

"Thank you." Bradley finds a seat before noticing the elderly couple staring at him with the same curiosity as the receptionist. He throws a smile and a nod their way.

After a few minutes pass, the waiting room door finally opens and the receptionist calls out, "Mr. Bulchovony? The doctor will see you now." The elderly man's wife places her hand underneath his left arm and assists in helping him up. They slowly disappear into the back offices.

Bradley finds himself alone in the waiting room. His anxiousness slowly grows as Jacob has already been waiting outside for roughly five, ten minutes. Before long, five minutes turns into ten, and ten turns into twenty. Bradley glances down at his watch. He becomes evermore worried that time is running out to be back at the diner for lunch as he promised.

Bradley happens to notice one of the photos sitting atop the escritoire near the far end of the anteroom. He approaches the photo and leans in for a closer observation. Seven men are present in the photo. Bradley assumes that one of them is Dr. Zehata, being that he's never actually seen the man. The rest of them however, are unfamiliar except one. One of the figures appears to be a younger looking Dr. Truax, but Bradley can't be sure.

Bradley checks his watch again. Time is running short. Just as

Bradley makes up his mind that this was a lost cause and turns to leave, the waiting room door suddenly opens and a short, partially baldheaded man steps out.

Bradley stops and begins his questionnaire. "Dr. Zehata?"

The bald man responds mildly, "What can I do for you, sir?"

"My name is Dr. Bradley Simpson. I was hoping we could speak for a few brief moments." Bradley approaches humbly, but Satieri is reluctant to engage. Satieri holds his ground without offering a handshake or even an introduction.

"What would you like to talk about, Dr. Simpson?" Satieri asks.

"First off, what can you tell me about this photo?" Bradley responds by pointing at the group of seven.

"That is a picture I took with The Medical Board of Trust." Satieri responds. "Why?"

"What can you tell me about *this* man?" Bradley points to the younger looking Truax.

Dr. Zehata looks at Bradley very abruptly. "Who are you? What do you want?"

"My name is Dr. Bradley Simpson. I work for St. John's Medical Center. I was the medical examiner for The Avenue massacre." Bradley detects a hint of hesitance on Satieri's part by this revelation.

Satieri's response, "That man is no one. I'm sorry Dr. Simpson, but I must return to my patients."

Satieri turns his back and goes to leave the waiting room when Bradley suddenly mutters, "I performed the autopsy on Mumahd's body. And his wife Saria."

Satieri stops. He slowly turns with his head tilted downward. As Satieri looks up at Bradley, he makes the request, "Please Dr. Simpson, follow me. Let's talk privately."

Bradley follows Satieri and they proceed through the waiting room door.

Dr. Zehata leads Bradley to a small office room. A wooden desk, a couple of office chairs, and a leather couch practically fill the area.

Two degrees bearing Satieri's name hang on the wall behind the desk. One is a Physical Doctrine in the field of medicine and the other is a Master's Degree in the field of science and technology. Bradley assumes they're both from The Indian Institute of Science because of the Hindi markings arranged on the certificates, but again, he can't be sure.

Dr. Zehata takes his seat behind the desk and begins explaining. "That photo was taken nearly thirty years ago. I spent a lot of my spare time doing scientific research with the partners you saw there. For over two decades, we dedicated ourselves to technological development that would usher in a new era of discovery and healing. In fact, I believe that photo was the last time we were all together. I left the lab after Mumahd was born."

Bradley still ponders about the identity of the one man. "Was that Truax in the picture?"

"Yes." Satieri responds.

"So Dr. Truax *was* on The Medical Board of Trust?" Bradley apparently didn't believe Walter.

"Dr. Walter Truax was one of our chief advisors. Everything we worked on needed approval for what they called practical use. It determined whether or not we'd receive the funding for development. Walter was very enthusiastic about our progress, but he always seemed to have a more sinister plot for our work. I never did trust his intentions."

Bradley decides to skip to the chase. "Why was Mumahd at the diner that day?"

Satieri seems somewhat uncomfortable talking about his son. He sighs and shifts his weight, procrastinating about the information. "Mumahd always did follow his own path. After he graduated, he was so proud of his accomplishments that he couldn't wait to come and work at my side. I was proud of him too. He worked for me for years, but after a while he seemed to steadily lose interest in being my assistant. He wanted more. It's strange, he reminds me of you. He started asking questions about my former lab partners, what we worked on, what was approved for development. I didn't want to tell him the truth."

Bradley interrupts, "What truth?"

Satieri rubs his forehead. Sweat has begun to bead over his face. Bradley isn't sure if it's because of his discomfort with the topic, or if it's from something more internal.

Satieri still continues, "The truth about their plans."

Bradley sits there confused and speechless, waiting on Dr. Zehata to cross the edifying threshold.

"What if I told you, Dr. Simpson, that the medical world is not out to cure you? What if I told you that their intentions are to keep you sick?"

Bradley doesn't understand. "There's new remedies prescribed all the time."

"They are stepping stones, Dr Simpson." Satieri proposes. "Minor advancements to simulate progress for the sake of public appeal. A way of keeping people locked into the ideal that one day all of our illnesses will cease to exist. How you say: throwing a dog a bone."

"What, like suppression over restoration? Beyond the cure?" Bradley knows far too well the rumors surrounding this concept.

"Exactly. To maintain the regiments interminably for mere job security." Satieri becomes increasingly more insecure.

Bradley holds onto his endearing nature to trust in faith. "I can't believe that. There have been so many people who've never succumbed to the symptoms where countless others have died."

"Then ask yourself, Dr. Simpson, what is the financial status of these so-called survivors?"

Bradley looks upwards trying to think of examples. "I would say middle to upper-class, I guess."

Satieri sets the record straight. "Money makes the world go round, Dr. Simpson. I tried explaining this to Mumahd, but it didn't matter. That was all he cared about. Not so much the achievement, just the life it offered. Once he rejoined my former colleagues and began to market our work, it was only a matter of time for someone like Tony Vicelli to get involved and monopolize the general distribution of these breakthroughs. I'm sorry Dr. Simpson, but you really have no idea of what you're getting yourself into."

Bradley is officially scared shitless now. He has been leaving very distinguishable footprints all over the medical realm in hopes of discovering the truth of one solitary drug. Now he understands why Dr. Pascoli encouraged his findings but within is own lingo of confidentiality.

Magnus was split into five subsidiaries, all with their own variety of prescription compounds that combat a range of diseases.

Bradley then reverberates, "So what was Mumahd's role at the diner?"

Satieri continues, "Mumahd was an ingenious scientist, and somewhat of an inventor too. The bugs were his idea. He spawned the idea from a reconnaissance program designed to imbed nano-robotics into sources of communications to gather audio and video intelligence. He thought that if the same procedures were taken toward the individual, it would render the intelligence aspect obsolete and create direct supervision. And he was right. No one would ever suspect the true architects. At least until you uncovered the truth."

Bradley wonders, "How can they afford the funding for these robots?"

Satieri almost snickers, "They don't. You do. It is all government funded, i.e. taxpayer's money."

"How can I stop them?" Bradley needs to reach out to anyone willing to help him. When taking on an entire corporation, or government for that matter, standing alone is the last thing you want.

Satieri doesn't respond right away. Instead, he leans his head down into the palms of his hands trying to comfort what appears to be a migraine.

Bradley shows concern. "Dr. Zehata? Are you all right?"

Satieri attempts to communicate while suppressing his anguish. "Dr. Simpson? What do you know of circuitry overload?"

Bradley remembers what the inspector said. "The Chief Inspector of the police mentioned Truax had been working on it for the last five years. A way for the bugs to withstand the overload."

Satieri offers the surprising remark, "Leonard knew from his adopted son Merrill that the pods could be deactivated. Let me ask you? Have you experienced symptoms of nausea, lightheadedness, a feeling of disorientation?"

Bradley lets out his own little secret. "Yes. Ever since Dr. Truax injected me at Mimi's place. Right before he gave the order to have her gunned down."

Dr. Zehata slowly unveils his covered face, lowers his hands, and braces his body in an attempt to stand. He nearly falls. Satieri must steady himself on the desktop to maintain balance. Bradley rises in an attempt to assist the weary doctor, but Satieri puts his hand out denying assistance. Satieri keeps his composure long enough to include, "Then you've been infected, Dr. Simpson. You must go now. Hide yourself. Hide your family. Any form of physical contact can distribute the bugs. Remember that."

Bradley insists, "What is circuitry overload?"

"How do you overload any type of circuit?" Suddenly, Satieri collapses on top of his desk. His upper torso smacks against the wooden surface and his head slumps to the side. However, his eyes remain open.

"Dr. Zehata!" Bradley rushes over to help the wounded doctor but Satieri's advice stops him.

Satieri continues lying atop the desk. He doesn't lift his head or even move a muscle as he speaks. "No! Get out of here. If you've already been infected, then the upgraded version of Neurolex is not in your system yet. Just go!"

Bradley quickly turns and heads toward the exit. He rips the door open before glancing back at Satieri one last time.

Dr. Zehata voices one final comment before Bradley leaves, "Good luck, Doctor." Bradley flees from the renowned physician's office.

Bradley decides to make a casual departure from Dr. Zehata's building. He doesn't wish to raise suspicion by fleeing the scene, knowing that Satieri is probably already dead by now, but a sense of urgency still compels him to keep pace. Bradley's sure they'll soon discover the truth, just as long as there are no witnesses who can identify his presence.

Bradley's casual pace however, crumbles at the sight of his watch. He has less than twenty minutes to be on time for lunch. Even Jacob confirms by his first question after Bradley enters the vehicle. "What took you so long?"

Bradley confesses, "I needed to gather some information. We can go now." Bradley backs out onto Main and drives off.

"We're going to be late for lunch." Jacob informs him.

"Only by a couple of minutes. We'll make up the time." Bradley's certainty is well understood by his son.

"Oh boy." Jacob reaches over, grabs the seatbelt, and buckles in. He knows his father's intentions, and even though it's not the Autobahn, Bradley will utilize the full extent of the interstate.

As they drive out of town, Jacob sneaks in the question, "What kind of information did you gather?"

Bradley tries evasive maneuvers, "Oh, nothing important. Just some medical stuff."

But Jacob isn't as gullible as Bradley thinks, "Was it about the murders?" he asks.

Bradley turns in shock at his son's accuracy. "What?"

Jacob alleviates the panic, "I can put two and two together, dad. You never want to visit grandma and grandpa, but you make us drive all the way down here, then you say we're going sightseeing, and then we end up here so that you can gather information on medical stuff? That's what WebMD is for. You're following leads again, aren't you?"

Bradley is at a loss for words, "Well, I didn't want to worry you," is all he can ever come up with.

Jacob persists, "It's all right. You can tell me."

Bradley gives in. He hates lying to his family. "Yes, Jacob. I came here to follow a lead. I needed to know why that guy's son was at the diner during the murders."

"What did you find out?" Jacob asks.

"Something very disturbing" Bradley replies. "I'll tell you later."

"Is it the bugs again?" Jacob has always been interested in cover-ups, espionage, and black ops. It explains why he chooses military enthused videogames.

Bradley honors Jacob's intrinsic supposition with a nod to acknowledge his acute perception. Bradley then adds, "Don't tell your mother. She'll have a cow."

Jacob assures his father. "Don't worry, I won't. Your secret is safe with me."

Our hero smiles in relief, thanks to the loyalty of his young partner in crime. "That's my boy."

CHAPTER 15

PHILADELPHIA BLUNDER (PART 2)

Bradley and Jacob pull up to the diner but the place is so packed that they have to park down the street a little ways.

Jacob spent most of the ride back inquiring about the details and progress of Bradley's detective work. And though Bradley averaged about ninety miles-per-hour during the venture, he still focused his good judgment enough to edit the story for content. He disclosed secrets regarding Phil's breakdown, Mimi's visitors betraying her, and finally how Satieri was executed via his preprogrammed hosts. Bradley felt his vivid descriptions might've been too much for his young son to bear, but Jacob reassured him that he's seen much worse violence in his videogames. (Not exactly reassuring.) Bradley was relieved that Jacob had an understanding of why culpability shouldn't be extracted in Bradley's favor and that a setup was more likely the intent.

The walk back to the diner consisted of formulating a verbal pact for prudence. Pinky swearing is so nineties.

Bradley and Jacob enter the diner to find that Marge, Roger, and Audrey have already ordered their entrees and are halfway finished by now.

"Where the *hell* have you been? I was worried sick." Is Audrey's greeting.

"Nice of you to join us." Is Marge's welcome.

And finally, "Out following leads again, huh?" Is Roger's stab. Count on Roger to add a little weight when someone's already walking on thin ice.

"What?" Audrey replies. "Is that why you brought us down here? To follow more leads? Let alone, you told my father?"

Considering that Bradley is in the hot seat now, he tries clambering about his rebuttal skills. Calmly and collectively he responds, "Uh, no. We just lost track of time. But thanks for that vote of confidence, guys."

Jacob continues on and takes his seat at the table. Marge is eager to acquire feedback on his experience. "So, how was sightseeing?" She asks.

"Not bad." Jacob responds. "The Liberty Bell is bigger than I thought it was." Jacob comes through in the clutch. Thankfully, since he studied historical landmarks in school, his detailed descriptions should help substantiate the duo's fabrication.

"Oh yeah? What else did you see?" Marge adds.

"Oh, City and Independence Hall. Our tour did run a little over. We saw the Art Museum, the Franklin Institute and its planet...?" Jacob turns to Bradley for confirmation.

"...planetarium. The Fels Planetarium." Bradley assists. He only recalls the name because Bradley himself always wished to visit the site as an excuse to avoid his in-laws during previous visits.

Jacob continues, "Yeah, that place. And I got to run up the same steps that Rocky ran up. It's not as easy as it looks in the movie."

Though Bradley is impressed, he actually feels bad that his devotion to investigating leads took precedent over Jacob's obvious desire for touring the attractions.

"Wow! You had quite the busy day." Marge says, concluding her quizzical extrapolation.

Bradley jumps in with a question to take some pressure off of Jacob, "How was shopping?"

Roger chuckles to himself while remaining engaged in his lobster bisque.

"Oh, not bad." Audrey speaks first. "We didn't really get much."

"Everything's so expensive anymore." Marge adds while she shares a harmless glance with her daughter.

"We just couldn't make up our minds." Audrey finishes.

But then Roger chimes in, "Yeah, on anything. All they did was complain. This is too revealing. This is too expensive. This is too lavender. I just sat back by the fountain tossing in coins. Hoping. Wishing. Maybe it would all end soon." Roger's comments are met with an eruption:

"I wasn't complaining!" "You complained more than we did!" "You didn't do anything!" "You could've helped!" "You just moped around!" "All their stuff was garbage anyways." "Their selection sucked!" "You got more than we did."

Roger suddenly interrupts, "I got a three-pack of tee shirts for five measly bucks. I can't just buy one, they only come in three's."

Bradley looks around the table at his wife, his mother-in-law, and his father-in-law all arguing back and forth. His son is laughing hysterically in observance of the adults assuming his own maturity level. And the entire restaurant has stopped eating long enough to observe the disturbance. Bradley finishes scanning over the intrigued crowd and refocuses his attention back on Roger's rundown expression.

Roger simply replies, "Welcome to my little slice of hell." He is well aware of the spectacle they just made, but embarrassment keeps him from turning to acknowledge his audience.

Just then, the waitress walks up to the table with a strange hint of reluctance. She planned without incident to take the newcomer's orders. Softly, she asks, "Can I get anyone anything?"

As smooth as silk, Bradley responds, "Yes. I'll take the corn beef sandwich with a side of fries, the coleslaw, and ranch dressing on the salad."

The waitress follows-up, "OK. And what to drink?"

Bradley can't hold back his ostentatious side any longer, "What's your strongest whiskey?"

Audrey hastily jumps in, "Bradley! Absolutely not."

Roger throws fuel on the flame, "Make it two."

Marge dives back in, "I don't think so, you're driving."

Just as another one of Audrey's and Marge's verbal eruptions is about to commence, Bradley quickly raises his hands and his voice declaring, "Whoa, whoa, whoa, whoa! Calm down. I was just kidding. I was going to say milkshake. I wanted a milkshake as my second choice."

"Really?" An unconvinced Audrey asks.

"Really?" A curious Jacob asks.

"Yeah. You want one?" Bradley responds to Jacob.

"Yeah!" Jacob might not have realized that his innocent enthusiasm broke down the unsocial quibbling, but again he came through in the clutch.

"What flavor are you thinking?" Bradley asks his son.

"Um, vanilla." Jacob places his order to the near weary waitress.

"I think I'll go with strawberry," says Bradley.

The waitress jots down their orders and turns back to Jacob. "And what to eat?" She seems somewhat comforted by speaking to the only one at the table with reserve.

"Chicken fingers." Jacob responds.

"Good choice." The waitress replies with encouragement while finalizing the orders on her notepad. "Alright. That'll be right up." She takes the remaining menus from the table and proceeds into the kitchen.

Only a couple of minutes pass before the waitress returns with one vanilla and one strawberry milkshake for the two boys. With a delighted comradeship, Bradley and Jacob clang their glasses together in celebration over the days bogged down accomplishments. The detective and his young consignor enjoy the sweet success.

From that point on, the rest of the afternoon carries on quite peacefully.

That evening however, proved to be much more than anyone anticipated.

Bradley and Audrey rest on the living room couch after another one of Marge's gourmet meals. Jacob shares his presence in a nearby corner chair, but his attention resides in some dumb game on the cell phone. Roger eventually enters the room and takes his place at the emerald-green upholstered armchair positioned closest to the television set. And Marge finishes cleaning up the kitchen in time to join the bunch on the loveseat.

The evening news is about to begin, and though none of them have any great interest in watching, they do wish to catch the season premiere of N.C.I.S. that follows. Unfortunately, they won't get that far.

By the third story, after a deadly house fire and a pile-up on the highway, a familiar face appears on the television screen above two hyphenated dates that depict birth and death. Bradley shifts his weight as he recognizes the face of Dr. Satieri Zehata.

The news informs Bradley of Satieri's outstanding professional legacy and personal background, the innovations and breakthroughs of his research, popularity with the public, especially those without insurance, and finally, fellow partners and their achievements over the years. A former member of The Medical Board of Trust, a naming of Satieri's ex-colleagues sends chills down Bradley's spine. The sudden information makes him uneasy almost to the point of being ill as the names of the renowned physicians are read: Dr. Charles Mendel, his understudy Dr. Walter Truax, Dr. André Broussard, Dr. Kenneth Johnston, and Dr. Anthony Vicelli. One final name is unfamiliar to Bradley: Dr. Vernon Borges. The seven men in Satieri's photo have been identified.

Tony Vicelli however, was never formally recognized as a doctor.

Audrey notices Bradley's uneasiness by the sudden squirming around on the couch for comfort. After confirming he's fine, Bradley realizes his nervous state has resurfaced the symptoms of fatigue and disorientation. As he tries to maintain focus, the news-cast gets worse.

The cause of death for Dr. Satieri Zehata is being deemed a mystery. A man with a perfect medical history doesn't simply fall over and die. Witnesses reported seeing a beige Mercedes SUV exit the doctor's office shortly before his body was discovered. According to the receptionist, the driver entered the locally owned practice and asked if he could speak with Dr. Zehata. She gave his name simply as, Dr. Simpson.

Bradley's in deep shit now.

Audrey snaps her head towards him. "What the hell did you do?"

"Nothing." Bradley insists.

"Nothing? Are you shitting me?" Audrey shakes her head with the realization, "So that's what you did all day? I should've known you didn't come here to sightsee. Not only that, but now you're involving our son in all this? Are you really *that* caught up on this conspiracy theory bullshit of yours?" Audrey stands from her spot on the sofa. "I can't believe you lied to me."

Bradley reports, "I didn't mean to lie to you. I needed to know what Dr. Zehata knew about Truax."

Roger quickly interrupts, "Dr. Walter Truax? As in the chief physician of N.E.T.I. Pharmaceuticals? The man they just mentioned?"

"One in the same," Bradley reassures.

Audrey maintains an unsure gaze on her capricious husband. She simply asks him outright, "Did you kill that man?" Audrey waits on a response.

"No, I didn't. Dr. Zehata had been infected for a long time." Bradley explains and continues, "They knew I was there. They wanted Satieri to tell me about The Medical Board of Trust and what they were working on. They waited till I was there to activate his program."

"Whose they?" Audrey inquires.

"Dr. Truax and the other execs of Magnus's subsidiaries. They seem to be able to track each infected host." Bradley reaches for support but can tell by the stunned faces of his audience that it will not come easily.

"How?" Audrey maintains her need for an explanation.

"I don't know." Bradley admits. "Some higher form of communication. Satellites, maybe."

Suddenly, Roger decides to add a very pertinent question. "What do you mean by activating the program of the infected hosts?"

Audrey can tell that Roger's question makes Bradley uncomfortable, so she chooses to reveal the conspiracy theory for him. "Bradley thinks the government is in league with the drug corporations and that they're putting microscopic robots in pills to manipulate our bodily functions."

Audrey's revelation quiets the room. An eagerness for a practical resolution looms over the living room. Everyone waits for some else to speak first.

Roger breaks the awkward silence with a statement, "Bradley? I think that you and I need to schedule a series of sessions." Roger is now convinced that Bradley suffers from some sort of postmortem stress and his overexposure conceded this paranoia driven illusion.

Audrey, calmly but firmly suggests, "No. I think that you have to leave. I'm sorry, honey, but this obsession of yours has put all of us in harm's way. And of all things, your son. You involved your son in a murder. And what if you're right? What if these things *do* exist and you've exposed him? You're not even taking into consideration the people around you."

Bradley tries to defend his case. "I'm trying to keep you from harm's way."

"No." Audrey does not allow Bradley the chance. "If this conspiracy is something you feel you have to uncover, then go and figure it out. I will no longer allow you to subject this family to your tunnel vision. I'm not going to wait till you get one of us hurt, or worse, killed."

"But, Audrey?" Bradley is very much surprised by his wife's

seriousness. But even Bradley has to admit, this investigation as taken on a very odd toll.

"I'm sorry, Bradley. I love you. But I want you out of here." Audrey begins to back out of the living room.

Bradley asks, "What about you and Jacob?"

"We'll be fine." Audrey responds. "We're going to stay here until all of this is over. You can take the truck. I just...can't deal with this anymore." Audrey turns and walks out of the living room and heads upstairs.

Bradley just sits there with a stunned compunction.

Marge, likewise, has kept a solitary gaze away from the center of attention where she usually strives to command that very thing. Bradley attempts an affectionate glance in Marge's direction in hopes of support, but his outreach is shyly denied. It almost seems like Marge has something to say but refuses to let go of her anonymity.

Bradley, being the source of tension, slowly stands up from the sofa and makes his way over to the coat rack in the kitchen. Jacob speaks to his father as his only supporter. "But, dad?"

"It's all right, Jakey. I'll be fine. You look after your mother." Bradley says while pulling his arms through the long sleeves of the hooded jacket.

"I will." Jacob replies.

As Bradley prepares to leave, he realizes, "What about my clothes?"

Audrey, having already foreseen this junction, marches down the steps with Bradley's suitcase in hand. She exclaims, "I figured you might need a change of clothes eventually."

"You read my mind," is Bradley's response.

"Here. I packed the hairdryer. I know you don't like having your hair wet." Audrey hands Bradley his suitcase and adds, "Be careful. Don't take the fall for all of this."

"Don't worry, I won't. I love you." Bradley leans in and kisses his wife. Audrey returns the affection.

Bradley turns to leave while telling Jacob, "We'll see you later, Jakey. Be good."

Jacob finalizes the departure by adding, "Whether in prison or not, dad, watch your ass."

"Jacob!" Audrey turns to her son.

"Thanks. I will." Bradley can't help but crack a smile on his face as he opens the backdoor and exits the house.

Bradley walks out into a cold, crisp night. The quietness of the neighborhood reminds Bradley that he's now on his own. The last place he wanted to be.

Bradley hops into the SUV and backs down the driveway. He decides not to head back home tonight, and that a nice, unassuming hotel room would prove to be a much safer decision. Bradley drives off into the night.

Meanwhile elsewhere...

A beeping alarm activates, warning the nearby systems operator that an unauthorized breach has been made. The operator slides his chair over to the adjacent console and queues a response. On the computer screen appears a satellite view of the United States. A small, red marker dots the eastern seaboard. As the operator types in further commands, a series of triangulated coordinates locate the violation and zoom in for identification processing.

The operator turns from the monitor and engages the intercom system, "Sir, it appears that Satellite L3 has detected movement from one of our tracked couriers," he casually exclaims.

"Which mark?" replies the small speaker box centered on the control panel.

The operator responds, "17190. He broke his signal radius again."

"Oh for crying out loud." The speaker answers. "Alright. I'm on my way."

A few moments later, Dr. Truax enters the operations room. Instead of his lab coat however, he's wearing his robe. He apparently wasn't planning on working much longer. Walter walks up to the operator and focuses on his computer monitor. "Where is he going?" he asks.

"I don't know. But it's pretty late to go for a drive," replies the operator.

Walter then asks, "Is he alone?"

"I'm not sure." the operator admits. "He's been all over the grid all day long. He's up to something."

"He's seeking information." Walter turns away from the monitor and puts his hand on the operator's shoulder before he says, "Dr. Bradley Simpson has become too great a liability. Execute his host program."

Dr. Truax then turns to exit the room as the operator asks one final question, "What's he seeking information on?"

Without turning or slowing his stride, Dr. Truax replies, "On us."

CHAPTER 16

CIRCUITRY OVERLOAD

Bradley pulls into the parking lot of the Red Roof Inn. The dull, orange glow of area lighting surrounds yet isolates the parking lot. Having already paid for his night, Bradley pulls his SUV nearest to the stairwell that leads to his second floor room and exits the vehicle. Capping an end to an already long and unexpected afternoon, Bradley ascends the stairs with suitcase in hand, makes his way over to number 207, and enters for the night.

Bradley flips the light switch to reveal the room is nothing too fancy. A lone, full-sized bed sits to the left with nightstands on both sides and lamps resting atop each stand. A twenty-seven inch flat screen television centers the room on the right while a small economy kitchen lays straight back on the left. The door leading to the bathroom is back on the right. Bradley drops his suitcase on the bed and sits down on the edge of the mattress. He takes a moment to observe his new surroundings and allow the gravity of this situation to be absorbed. Bradley finally releases a nervous sigh, rubs his still aching head, and glances down at the remote for the TV. He decides to untie his shoes, sit back, relax, and watch a little boob tube.

Bradley stands up from the bed and makes his way over to a series of coat hooks by the door to take off his jacket. He hangs his coat before grabbing a nearby chair from the corner and taking a seat to remove his loafers. Bradley then takes his suitcase from the bed and replaces it with his spot on the chair before reaching for the remote and comfortably laying back in the bed. While putting his feet up, Bradley clicks the remote and as the picture fades into focus, Bradley crosses his arms behind his head and positions himself for a soporific evening.

Unfortunately, the static feedback from the television almost instantly resurfaces his symptoms of fatigue and nausea. Bradley closes his eyes in an attempt to cope with the discomfort. He inhales through his nose and exhales through his mouth, as would anyone suffering from nervous anxiety. As the discomfort increases, Bradley squirms more and more from his bed down position until he's again sitting up on the edge of the mattress. Bradley suddenly leans over, grabs the nearby waste basket, and vomits.

Bradley eventually gathers his composure. He wipes the beads of sweat from his brow with his sleeve and turns back to observe the door leading to the bathroom. Bradley decides to clean up his act, and possibly brush his teeth. Before turning off the TV, he takes a small travel bag, a change of clothes, and the hairdryer from the suitcase and then makes his way into the bathroom.

After a while...The shower water comes to a halt in the now steamed over stall of the small hotel bathroom. Bradley pulls the curtain aside and reaches for the towel hanging nearby. He wraps his waist and steps out onto the cold linoleum. Bradley swipes his hand across the vanity mirror to remove the condensation and takes a look at his face. To Bradley's surprise, the blacks of his eyes have shrunken to pinholes and the overpowering blue of his retinas alert Bradley to the seriousness of his deteriorating condition.

Though the hot shower somewhat aided in Bradley's fatigue, he still moves apprehensively. He glances down at the hairdryer resting on the counter beside the sink. Bradley plugs the cord into the wall socket and decides to dry his hair.

When Bradley turns on the hairdryer, the electrical circuitry bridges the connection from the device to the static in his body. The response triggers the already activated bugs to quickly execute their lethal program. They attach themselves to their designated nerve system within the good doctor's brain and commence electrical output orders upon their host.

Bradley can't focus. He can see the lateral palpebral ligaments underneath his eyes involuntarily twitching. His mind goes numb and he begins to seizure. The hairdryer shakes and its motor whines as Bradley's head and upper body violently convulse. He slams his hands down against the edge of the sink and tries to steady his balance. Bradley can't center his reflection while he looks in the mirror and tries to will self-control over his movements and line of sight. The pain is too great.

A sudden shock stings Bradley in the hand. He looks down to see that the handle of the hairdryer has been smashed and his fingers have come to rest over its exposed wires.

Bradley then remembers what Dr. Zehata said: Circuitry overload. He grasps a hold of the bare copper and accepts the one hundred and twenty-five volts. Bradley quickly drops the hairdryer and jumps back in pain. Unfortunately, the partial electrocution delays but does not alleviate his dilemma. Dr. Simpson is running out of options.

Bradley then decides on an ingenious and ultimately idiotic solution. The thirty-two year old medical examiner picks up the damaged hairdryer, opens his mouth wide, leans in close, and bites down on the exposed wires as hard as he can. The electricity courses through his enamel and into the cranial cavity frying nerve receptors and their endings, thus causing his jaw to lock and his muscles to tense. Dr. Bradley Simpson's body goes stiff and falls backwards, hitting hard off the floor. He lies motionless.

Miles away...in the stronghold of the surrounding foothills, the N.E.T.I. Pharmaceuticals headquarters receives a sudden distress alert from their allied network. One of their host's courier signals was suddenly terminated, which only occurs if the host ceases to emit functional brain waves implying that they've recently died or have been executed. Another arbitrary systems monitor approaches the alarmed computer and uploads the incoming. As the triangulated disturbance is pinpointed and its designation and location appears on the screen, the satellite phone that centers the panel begins to ring. The operator depresses the button to the switchboard and responds.

Dr. Truax curiously imposes on the occurrence, "What happened?"

The operator replies, "Nothing. We lost the signal to one of our couriers."

"Which one?" Truax asks.

"SL3-17190."

Walter responds, "Thank you very much. That's good news. You may continue." Walter disconnects the transmission and takes a step back from his desk and computer console. "Goodbye, Dr. Simpson."

Still wearing his robe, Dr. Truax slowly turns and makes his way over to the sofa bed in the corner of his office and lies down. Walter closes his eyes for a good night's sleep.

Back at the hotel...

A soft, steady chirp fills the background as beads of water leak from the bathroom faucet and drip down into the overflowing sink bowl. A small layer of water has accumulated on the white linoleum floor where the body of Dr. Simpson continues to lie.

Flashes of light begin to interrupt the darkness as the recovering doctor starts blinking his way back to consciousness. Bradley opens his eyes to find he's lying in a substantial puddle on the floor. The short-circuited hairdryer lies beside him, still plugged into the wall socket. Bradley wonders how many times he might have been electrocuted before the appliance finally fried its motor. Nonetheless, he rolls over onto his side, positions his arms underneath his body, and attempts to lift himself. After a few weary tries, Bradley manages to get up on his knees. He takes a moment to gather his strength.

With assistance from the sink top, Bradley eventually pulls himself up to his feet and is able to stand. He takes a glimpse in the mirror and is relieved to see that his eyes have since dilated and his symptoms seem to have abated.

Then it all comes to him: Circuitry overload. The sudden surge of power when properly directed, overloads the computing power of the pods and (like tripping a breaker) electronically disables the system. Bradley has finally figured out the fatal flaw of the original compound that prompted a five year redevelopment procedure for the now upgraded Neurolex. Once again, our hero endures.

Having regained most of his equilibrium, Bradley manages to reach the bathroom door and step out into the living room. He makes his way into the small economy kitchen and pulls a drinking glass from the cupboard before turning back to the faucet. Bradley twists the handle and takes a moment to enjoy a nice cold drink.

Realizing he conquered his symptoms, Dr. Simpson goes back to his original plan: try to sit back and relax. And thus, his comfortable evening is victorious.

CHAPTER 17

REINSTAD CONSPIRACY

Bradley wakes up rather early, not being able to settle comfortably during the night. He pokes around the hotel room for a while, tending to his presence from the night before, and then decides to get dressed. Before long, the good doctor gathers his things, departs from this depressing dwelling, and checks out early. But not before heading down to the dining area for his free continental breakfast. After choking down a few cups of coffee and half of a banana bread muffin, Bradley pulls out his laptop to take advantage of the hotel's Wi-Fi network in order to recommence his investigation. The final target: Terra Reinstad.

Terra Monique Reinstad is from a family of entrepreneurs. Her parents, George and Sharon Reinstad, run their own law practice which represents interests in both high value residential and commercial properties. Proud defendants against varieties including insurance, mortgage, and tax fraud, they've forged the Reinstad Law Firm into the eighth largest firm in accordance to assets in the country. Only working with major estates and Fortune 1000 companies certainly paid its dividends.

Terra's older brother, David Reinstad, owns a small chain of three successful delis located near the epicenters of their respective cities. David's name actually appears on a lease application for the building where The Avenue now lies, but venues in New York, Chicago, and Cleveland prove to be a demanding enough responsibility for the thirty-seven year old.

Terra's younger brother, Benny Reinstad, lives out west and runs his own talent agency which represents forms of artistry that includes acting, both theatrical and screen, various forms of writing, all musical interests, and freelance fashion/wardrobe design.

Twenty-eight year old Terra had no children nor had ever been married. For the last four years, Terra had worked as a financial consultant under the insurance giant, Mutual Comprehensive: Loans and Subsidies. Her last known address was her parent's estate located at 7889 Heritage Court. However, Heritage Court doesn't show up anywhere among the public domain. In essence, it doesn't exist.

Bradley seems to be up against all odds. He'll have to dig a little deeper if he's to make progress on this last lead. He finally looks up from his laptop and realizes that he's now alone in the dining room. Two hotel workers stand aside and anxiously await their opportunity to bus the last remaining table. Without even so much as Bradley's knowledge, everyone ate, digested their overabundance, and left to continue on with their day. Next, please.

Bradley collects his belongings, makes his way outside, and prepares the SUV for the journey home. The journey home isn't fraught with such scenic obstructions as the initial excursion, nor the time it takes to stop for bathroom breaks or a quick lunch.

Bradley drives straight home, not stopping for anything. The rushed pace actually shaves a good hour off his e.t.a. He pulls onto the street that leads home, and before he can even pull in the driveway, he notices an unknown charcoal sedan parked in the approach. Bradley finally remembers the owner of the sedan when he pulls up next to it and the driver's side door is a different color from the rest of the car, being it was just recently replaced. Detective Paige Dunbar exits her vehicle and waits for Bradley to do the same.

Bradley exits his vehicle and opens with the question, "What can I do for you, Detective?"

The detective responds, "Welcome back, Dr. Simpson. I was just about to take off. I didn't know when you'd be home."

Bradley exclaims, "Oh, I'm certainly back now."

Paige surprises Bradley with her next question, "How was Trenton? Did you learn anything new?"

"How did you know I went to Trenton?" Bradley asks.

"Well unfortunately, that's why I'm here." Paige explains. "I'm supposed to place you under arrest. When your name was dropped during the newscast of Dr. Zehata's death, the Captain traced your cell phone and the onboard GPS in your truck, to find you were at or somewhere near the scene of the crime. He immediately issued a warrant for your arrest. I was ordered to bring you in."

Bradley in turn, surprises Paige with his comment, "I can't, Detective Dunbar. I'm sorry. I have to follow one more lead."

"And that's also why I came," offers Paige. "I figured you might find something else to go on. What is it? What did you learn?"

Bradley catches the detective up to speed. "I learned I grossly underestimated just how widespread Neurolex and similar compounds have become incorporated into our drug market. I learned that The Medical Board of Trust has been in development of these compounds for the greater part of thirty years. And I found out that Dr. Charles Mendel's niece, Terra Reinstad, has no known place of residence except for an estate that's located on a street which doesn't exist. Other than that, I learned how to electrocute myself with a hairdryer."

"Oh, that sounds nice." sarcastically remarks Paige. "What is this address that doesn't exist?"

Bradley replies, "7889 Heritage Court. Her parents, George and Sharon Reinstad live there."

"Heritage Court?" Paige asks while attempting to resurface her memory bank. "I know where that is. It's up in the foothills off of Sycamore Grove."

Bradley is starting to notice a pattern forming. "Of course it is. Why didn't I already know that?" Everyone who's been directly involved with this case has a residence in the foothills, almost like they're all cronies. The proverbial bough has to break at one point.

Paige gets right on it, "Well, if that's our next destination. Then we better get to it."

Bradley is somewhat comforted by his allegiance with the good detective. The last thing he wanted was to be on his own, and the detective acts as the perfect buffer in which even Bradley's own wife will not consign. It's good to have friends in high places.

Heritage Court is not actually a road after all. Bradley left his SUV behind and they ascended the foothills in Paige's sedan. Where Sycamore Grove ends, a gigantic lot opens to form Heritage Court. Three estates are spread out within the lot and formally hidden by the cover of the surrounding tree line, the Reinstad place being one of them.

Three separate gates guard the entrance to each estate. Voice boxes are located near the gates for purposes of identification and entry approval. The name REINSTAD is forged into the iron gate that centers the lot.

Detective Dunbar pulls up to the corresponding entry console and presses the call button. A voice comes over the speaker box, "Who is it?"

Paige responds, "Detective Paige Dunbar. I need to speak with George Reinstad."

The voice replies, "I'm sorry, Mr. Reinstad isn't in."

The detective doesn't plan on being turned away from this hurdle in the investigation. She quickly asks, "Well, is Sharon Reinstad available?"

But again, the voice confirms, "Misses Reinstad isn't in either."

Detective Dunbar won't be denied any longer. She goes straight for the jugular. "I'm here concerning the death of their daughter, Terra Reinstad. If you would like, I could go get a search warrant so that we can properly continue this investigation. But I'm sure we could look past all that if you're willing to cooperate."

After a few moments of silence, a different sounding voice comes over the speaker and says, "You may enter, Detective Dunbar. And please, bring your friend with you."

Surprised, Paige turns and looks at Bradley wondering how the voice knew of his presence. She looks back at the entry console and inspects the panel for a possible camera. Meanwhile, the iron gate automatically retracts to allow the visitors admission. The charcoal sedan enters the estate and advances down the tree lined lane.

The estate's property opens up after about one hundred yards to reveal a large mansion consuming its acreage. The lane shadows a couple of small, private golf holes while an expansive view of the foothills looms in the distance. A guest house sits off to the right nestled against the surrounding forest line. Detective Dunbar pulls around to the front of the house and parks the car. Paige and Bradley step out of the vehicle in time to meet the butler as he exits the front doors.

The butler quickly descends the front steps and offers his greeting, "Welcome, Detective Dunbar. If there's anything you need, just ask." The butler then turns to Bradley. "And, Mr. ...?"

Since Bradley takes pride in his title, he responds, "It's Doctor, actually. Doctor Bradley Simpson."

The butler respectably replies, "Excuse me, Doctor. Welcome." The butler then opens his arms and motions toward the entrance. "If the both of you would please, follow me." The butler turns and heads back into the estate while Bradley and Detective Dunbar share a smirking glance before slowly following the chief servant.

The Reinstad estate is a model of modern engineering. Large energy efficient windows surround the structure and allow natural light into every room in which case, electrical lighting becomes irrelevant until nighttime. Coupled by solar panels and various wind driven turbines identifiable by the large panes of black glass and small propeller systems that dot the roof, which are both eventually hard wired into the main as a fault interrupter, as well as the network of landscaped channels that redirect water into another hydroelectric basin, the estate is essentially self-sustaining. (Not bad for a bunch of half-assed mountain boys.)

The interior boasts an exquisite modern design with high, curved ceilings and art covered walls all colored in some shade of light gray or off-white. A state-of-the-art computer networked communications, entertainment, and security systems access panel in every room. Hardwood flooring covers the main corridors, tile flooring accents the kitchen, plush carpeting laid in the living room, and Nature Stone flooring literally, everywhere else. (Imaginative repetition. Go figure.)

Other than that, everything looks really clean and neutral. Even if the beauty of traditional wood trim accents has been replaced with the more futuristic chrome or tungsten shaded metallic décor that's accompanied by glass shelving, table tops, and cabinet fronts. Gray is the new blue.

As Bradley and Detective Dunbar are escorted through the spacious, overarched, and inanimate house, Bradley can't help but feel that he's in the lair of the world's evilest science nerd. The butler works quickly through the house, navigating beyond the central reception area, taking a short hallway into the kitchen, passing through the connected Nature Stone sunroom, and out onto the back veranda.

Bradley and the detective follow the butler down a flight of concrete steps onto the main terrace. A large, in ground pool centers the terrace while an additional flight of concrete steps descend to the ground level. The yard beyond is ornamented with multiple flower gardens that form general walkways throughout the grounds.

Beside the pool on the main terrace, two men side at an umbrella covered patio table while nearby on the corner of the terrace, a third man stands inside the pagoda bar preparing a drink. The butler leads his guests over to the table for proper introductions.

"Gentlemen, may I present to you, Detective Paige Dunbar and Dr. Bradley Simpson." The butler offers a bow to his masters as well as his guests, and then quickly turns and departs from this disclosure in which he's inadequate of its designation.

One of the unknown men simply replies, "Thanks, Luther."

Bradley notices an eerie similarity to the two strangers sitting before him with something from his past. His premonition is soon satisfied when one of them removes his sunglasses. Bradley stares in shock as the once dead Dr. Charles Mendel stares back at him very much alive.

Dr. Mendel opens with playful derision, "Why Dr. Simpson, you look as if you've seen a ghost." Charles turns and shares a laugh with his still unknown sidekick. Bradley can't seem to pinpoint the other man's identity, but he's sure they've met before.

Dr. Mendel glances back at Bradley, then decides to break the ice, "I'm sorry, where are my manners? Dr. Simpson, Detective Dunbar, my name is Dr. Charles Mendel, and may I introduce you to Dr. Kenneth Johnston." Mendel looks upwards trying to remember, "He was our number four guy in the Trust."

Dr. Johnston quickly corrects, "I was the number three guy, Charles."

"That's right, he was our number three guy." Mendel confidently asserts his inaccuracies.

Since Dr. Johnston shares the same careless leisure as his partner, that plus the eleven a.m. margaritas they're consuming, he responds quite mischievously. He asks Dr. Mendel, "Are you off your meds again?"

"How could I forget?" Mendel remarks.

Dr. Mendel and Dr. Johnston soak up their social and administrative immunity in childish regard. They notice Bradley is still staring at them with this stunned look of disbelief. Dr. Mendel finally asks, "Is everything OK, Dr. Simpson?"

All Bradley can mutter is, "I performed an autopsy on you."

Mendel responds, "Yes, you did. And I thank you. You were very gentle." Charles and his coerce share another laugh. Their behavior reflects two children who enjoy hiding sworn secrets from ignorant eavesdroppers.

While the juvenile doctors elate, Bradley and Paige observe the third member of the gathering return from the bar and join in the fun. His presence revokes more feelings of confusion and disbelief.

As the unknown man approaches, Paige leans over to Bradley and whispers in his ear, "I know that man." And just as Bradley is about to inquire the details, the unknown figure speaks.

"Detective Dunbar? Dr. Simpson? It's a pleasure to meet you. My name is Antonio Vicelli. But you can call me, Tony." Tony Vicelli reaches out his hand with a formal gesture, but the guests are somewhat bewildered and don't take to the greeting right away. Bradley finally commences the introductory handshake and therefore sets Tony's next comments in motion. "Please, have a seat. You'll have to forgive my colleagues, their manners are selective."

Dr. Mendel defends his social graces, "I was just about to offer them a seat."

"I thought we were awfully forthcoming." Dr. Johnston assists.

Tony takes the lounge chair beside his friends and co-conspirators while Dr. Simpson and Detective Dunbar choose two seats on the opposing side of the table. "Would you care for a drink?" Offers Tony, as he sets three glasses filled with ice and some red colored concoction down on the table.

Bradley slowly complies, "You know what? I think I would."

"Bradley!" Detective Dunbar scolds Bradley's unaccountability similar to the way his wife would.

"That's the spirit." Tony slides one of the drinks toward Bradley before turning to Detective Dunbar. "And you, Detective?"

"No. Thank you. Someone has to drive." Paige firmly declares.

"Suit yourself." Tony takes a sip from his glass while Dr. Mendel reaches for the other drink.

Mendel shares his prerogative, "I only drive after I've had a couple drinks. It takes the edge off."

And thus, the introductions have been made and the libations shared, but the lack of conversation on the visitor's part sparks Tony to take command over the interaction. He starts by putting the ball in Bradley's court. "You look like you have something on your mind, Dr. Simpson?"

Since Bradley can't place the possibilities of this puzzle fast enough, he simply remarks, "How are you all still here?"

Dr. Mendel quickly relishes the opportunity, "I live here."

Dr. Johnston follows, "I live over there." Kenneth points east toward the tree line which conceals the neighboring estate.

And Tony finalizes, "Mine's that way." Vicelli points west toward his neighboring estate. They're cronies after all.

Tony continues, offering the next topic, "Which reminds me, Dr. Simpson. How are *you* still here? I heard your program signal had been terminated."

Bradley responds with pride, "I performed a circuitry overload."

All three men respond in the same way and at the same time. "Ouch!" Bradley is suddenly hit with a barrage of playful admiration.

Dr. Johnston strikes first, "How did you do yours?"

Bradley can't believe that he's actually engaging in this seemingly sadistic topic, but the bread crumbs must be followed. He answers Dr. Johnston, "I bit down on the exposed wires of a hairdryer."

Once again, his audience responds in harmony, "Ouch!"

"Did it stop your heart?" asks Dr. Mendel.

"Only for a moment. I blacked out after I hit the bathroom floor." Bradley relaxes enough to enjoy the first sip of his mixed drink.

Dr. Mendel then makes a curious remark, "Yeah, I pissed myself the first time. I used a defibrillator though."

As the men share another laugh, Dr. Johnston reveals his procedure, "I used a car battery."

Tony gives his personal opinion, "I think Detective Dunbar has the best method at her disposal."

Being that Paige has no idea what any of them are talking about, she purely exclaims, "What the hell are you guys talking about?"

Bradley leans over, "Circuitry overload."

Vicelli continues on with his revelation, "Your TASER gun, Detective. It can be applied to any part of the body, directly conveying the electricity into the affected host."

Paige asks, "Again, what the hell are you guys talking about?"

Bradley reconfirms, "Circuitry overload."

This time, Paige leans over to Bradley, "No shit. I heard you the first time. What does that mean?"

Dr. Mendel jumps in, "It means you have to electrocute yourself to find out."

Tony can tell they're getting nowhere fast, so he decides to regain mastery over the conversation. "Circuitry overload means exposing yourself to an electrical circuit in order to fry the surveillance device that we've manufactured to attach itself to vital nerves within your body, Detective Dunbar. It's really not that complicated."

"No shit." Paige responds. "So Bradley was right?"

Dr. Mendel jumps at her informality, "Bradley? We've blossomed to a first name basis, have we?"

After a moment of blushing and a good dose of humility, the detective corrects herself, "I meant, Doctor. So Dr. Simpson was right?"

Tony answers, "Detective, you have no idea." Vicelli enjoys a sip of his drink and the suspense before he continues. "In nineteen forty-six, the United States government introduced a collection of recovered documents and scientific technologies from various parts of Nazi Germany and war torn Europe. Among these documents, there were a considerable amount of proposed advancements in the field of medical treatment. After Oppenheimer's demonstration, the government sought out scientific novelties as a nationalistic playing card. A subtle precursor to the Cold War. Eventually, a panel of experts were assembled, not so much in the interest of rebuilding or reverse engineering, we were already making our own breakthroughs, but more to establish or adapt a real-world practicality for the means of industry, manufacturing. We wanted to offer solutions to the world's problems."

Bradley interrupts, "And so it led to the development of micro-scopic assassins?"

Tony grants a sigh toward his intolerance for interludes, stares at Bradley, and then resumes. "It took the advent of transistors, and later the microprocessor, for us to realize the possibilities. After Hoover went ape-shit on security reconnaissance, we knew the future of imbedding bugs would advance rapidly. So as satellites went up, and infrared sensors were implemented, and the world-wide-web was built around this grand communications network, all the while medical applications were also being explored and incorporated. Sadly, it took another three decades for the Trust to gain a scientific solution that was applicable. And even then, the inevitable glitch of circuitry overload was just waiting in the wings."

Dr. Mendel chooses to interrupt with a strange comment, "Yeah, too bad Merrill couldn't hide forever."

But then Dr. Johnston adds to the self-incrimination, "The Zehata family value didn't fair much better."

As Tony looks down into his glass trying to hide the smile on his face, he shifts his weight before continuing, "Thanks to a panel of dedicated experts at our disposal, we're able to see our hard work pay off."

Now Bradley remembers why he's here. One simple question has dragged him down a chain of dangerous and disconcerted events, and with that question, Dr. Simpson takes lead. "Then why the massacre at The Avenue? Why split Magnus apart?"

Tony responds, "For the royalties, Dr. Simpson. Five companies are better than one. Plus, this way we can ensure proper product placement."

Bradley begins to unhinge from Tony's laid-back composure. "Is that why you had everyone murdered? They didn't agree with your product placement? Is that why Eugene is dead? Is that why Merrill and Mimi were shot? Is that why Satieri, Mumahd, Saria, and her unborn child were killed? Why your own daughter was executed?" Bradley turns and focuses on Dr. Johnston. "Is that why you had your son murdered?" Bradley then turns to Dr. Mendel, "How you're not dead, I still don't know."

Tony and his band of deceivers start to mellow out amidst the detailed critique. Kenneth Johnston defends his decision first, "Miles is dead because he didn't possess the mindset to carry the company forward."

"What!" Detective Dunbar chimes in. "So that's all it takes?"

Dr. Johnston nods with a slight shrug in his shoulders, "Well yeah, pretty much."

Dr. Mendel offers his two cents, "Technically, I was never dead."

"What the hell does *that* mean?" Bradley asks impatiently.

Tony interrupts to sooth the tensions, "Take it easy, Dr. Simpson. Just relax. You're far too overwrought. What Dr. Mendel means is that he staged his own death."

Bradley shares a confusing glance with Detective Dunbar before turning back to Tony. "How?" he asks.

Tony submits, "You think these bugs were only designed to harm. And with someone like Dr. Walter Truax involved, I can't blame you. He always was a little creepy. The truth however, is the exact opposite. Like I said, we wanted to offer solutions to the world's problems. Our first breakthrough came when we successfully revived a coma patient by implanting a neurological bridge of robotic transistors into the host's brain stem." Tony actually curls his fingers while saying transistors. "You see, the bugs only respond to an electrical source, in this case your nervous system. The greatest information superhighway known to man. The bugs assist in the conveyance of neurological signals to inhibit or enhance physical response. When you performed your gentle autopsy on Dr. Mendel here..."

Dr. Mendel smiles and lowers his glasses to wink at Bradley while Tony speaks.

"...his body was simply turned off. No heartbeat, no brain activity, all deemed inanimate to evoke circuitry overload."

Bradley sneaks in the question, "What about his bullet wound?"

Tony sustains his leverage, "You addressed his bullet wound, you didn't actually dress it. That wound was given by us the morning of the massacre. It was cosmetic."

Bradley is confused now more than ever. If Dr. Mendel was killed by the sudden electrical output of the pods, then how did they bring him back to life?

Bradley listens as Tony continues educating. "Electrocuting yourself doesn't create the circuitry overload, it simply shuts down the pods. As a fail-safe to maintain our innocence from medical tampering, if the bugs lose their connection to an electrical source for more than twelve hours, the host is presumed dead and an overload occurs. The pods are designed to self-destruct and charge all the nerves throughout your body. So the reason you're still here, Dr. Simpson, is because the overload restarted your heart after your hair-raising experiment stopped it. In other words, you committed suicide. The bugs saved you by performing a procedure that was designed to kill you. You were on the floor of that hotel bathroom a lot longer than you think. Just the same way Dr. Mendel's heart was restarted in Dr. Grischow's office almost two days after your autopsy. That was actually Dr. Truax's contribution, with Mumahd's help of course. They found a way to emit an electromagnetic pulse that can activate the bugs as an emergency override without col-lapsing their circuit first. If you introduce too many pods within the host, they draw enough power to effectively shut down the brain. So, a contingency application was devised. As soon as the bugs are introduced, even before they assemble and attach to their desig-nated system, the pulse initiates their program orders and arms them for overload. But unfortunately, if you're already infected and are anywhere within the proximity of the blast, the pods will shut down your brain functions and probably stop your heart."

Dr. Mendel suddenly slaps his hands together and exults, "Boom! You drop like a fly."

Tony takes a long gulp from his drink and finalizes, "That's what brought everyone to The Avenue that day, Dr. Simpson. The five year upgrade to Neurolex, a compound called Equinox, was being unveiled to a board of skeptics, hippies, and idealists. Eugene and his bastard son Merrill wanted to make love with the world, not war. Tyler Vaughn was nothing short of a pussy. That's probably why him and Merrill shared relations. Apparently, Eugene didn't take too kindly to it though. He gave up Merrill when he was sixteen, not as a baby like you think, after he brought his new boyfriend home. Miles and Mumahd simply enjoyed their medical monopoly too much for the company's advancement interests. My dear daughter Karen, was only a bookworm. All she could do was crunch numbers. I offered her The Avenue but she wanted to be a partner. I knew that was too much for her to undertake. And the infamous, Dr. Charles Mendel, was shot by a blank. Our gunman was given explicit orders to keep count on who and when the shots would be fired."

Bradley interrupts confused, "But I thought *you* were the shooter?"

"No, Dr. Simpson." Tony now relishes. "That honor goes to my twin brother. The late, great, Dr. Anthony Vicelli. Also known as Tony."

Bradley's eyes widen and his mouth drops. The cover-up is all starting to make sense. "Dr. Anthony Vicelli from the Medical Board of Trust? Satieri's ex-colleague?" Bradley shakes his head in naivety. He then comments, "You killed your own brother."

Tony finally chooses to unveil his motive. "My brother was an idealist, Dr. Simpson. No matter how much patients begged him, no matter how many times he helped them, no matter how often he let them go without paying, without insurance, it was never good enough. All they did was bitch. Our practices, our policies, our prices, our response time. My incorruptible brother always wanted to help them. No matter what. He spent years working with the Trust in order to affect real change, and for what? To be criticized, decommissioned, and disregarded. He was a fool. And that's when I realized the simple truth: Americans, like most other nations, are spoiled by their expectations. They don't care how a product works, who built it, or how hard it was to develop. They just care that it works up to their expectations, that it costs in accordance to their expectations, and best of all, they all want it yesterday. So, I decided to consolidate my assets and begin buying off the Trust's private manufacturers. As the CEO of the nation's leading medical insurance company, I knew that once I had control over the facilities, the distributors would systematically follow to escape the market pinch. And though a monopoly was imminent, I didn't foresee all the softies that would end up working on our executive board. They knew far too well the gravity of this application and so decided it was not in the public's best interest. But here's the thing, no one ever said the public had to know about it."

Detective Dunbar can't hold back her feelings any longer, "You're a monster."

"Why, thank you." Tony tips his glass at Paige before consuming its remnants. "As far as my brother was concerned, we executed his host program. But unlike yours, Dr. Simpson, which was designed to shut down your brain, his was designed to accept orders for motive of operation. The pods sparked certain nerves to constantly remind him of his preprogrammed assignment. Unfortunately, since we knew how picky and precise you'd be in regards of your reputation and that you'd probably perform the autopsy long before the pods were designed to self-destruct, he kind of had to finish the job himself. But again, we were able to include that little detail into his program. Consequently though, it did leave the door open for the opportunity of their discovery. That's actually why you're here, Dr. Simpson. You're the last liability."

Bradley suddenly remembers the red circle that was drawn on Dr. Anthony Vicelli's throat. The doctor actually targeted a specific line where the bullet was to exit and create a pathway for the pod to leak out.

Though now greatly concerned over his well-being, Bradley follows up Tony's explanation with an important question. "You said you devised a contingency application for circuit collapse. What does that mean?"

Tony's face fills with joy and excitement over this revelation, "People rely on our compounds, Dr. Simpson. They have for decades now. Once an infected host's signal reaches standby for execution, the bugs have no further purpose in that particular host. So, if the patient continues their prescription plan as they should, the contingency application against overload redirects the bugs to external delivery sources. Like your hands. Or your lungs. Or even your clothing. That way, they can be spread to new hosts. It only takes about a quarter million bugs for us to establish a signal."

Bradley and Paige just stare in horror as they learn the truth. That's why Dr. Zehata didn't want Bradley to help him in Trenton. He didn't want to transmit his infection of the upgraded Neurolex.

Tony maintains diction, "Chances are, Dr. Simpson, Detective Dunbar, you've probably already come in contact with someone that's been infected. Cheers!" Tony lifts his empty glass and shares a toast with Dr. Mendel and Dr. Johnston. They all look at Bradley and wait for him to eventually join in, but it appears he doesn't care to partake in this particular celebration.

Bradley is absolutely mortified over their candid appreciation for such an achievement: A system of control that hides in the shadows and manipulates the very ignorance of mankind while hypocritically seeking their support to enable financial security.

And that's when Bradley realizes he might've subjected his own family to such a threat. Like Audrey said, he involved his son. Now Audrey and Jacob wait in Philadelphia alone, unprotected, and at risk of being victims of this sick plot. Bradley stands to leave. "I won't let you guys get away with this. I will stop you."

"No, Dr. Simpson, why don't you join us?" requests Tony as he reaches into his pocket and slides two pills across the table to Bradley. "Imagine a world without headaches. Without backaches. Without the common cold. Imagine a world without disease. Better yet, imagine a world without pain. Hell, before long we could engineer a world without death. You just take two of these and *don't* call me in the morning."

The threesome erupts with laughter over the irony while Bradley reaches down and urges Paige to leave with him. The detective stands and offers a warning, "Well, I suspect we'll be seeing you three real soon. Just as soon as I can get a warrant for your arrest."

Dr. Mendel deflects with charm, "Why Detective Dunbar, that's the most thoughtful thing you've said all afternoon. One thing you have to remember though, we're already dead. Good luck."

The three senile geniuses elate in their lackluster lifestyle while Dr. Simpson and Detective Dunbar start to walk away from the table. Tony Vicelli quickly intervenes, "And where are you going to go now, Dr. Simpson? Haven't you narrowed down your leads yet?"

Bradley turns and says, "I'm going to start from the beginning, Tony. With N.E.T.I. Pharmaceuticals."

Tony suddenly exclaims, "A man of strict and thorough analysis. Just like your father."

Bradley stops dead in his tracks and turns back to Vicelli, "What'd you just say?"

Tony answers by responding to Detective Dunbar, "Hey, Detective Dunbar? Let me ask you, since you know Bradley so well, does he ever mention his infamous parents? You should ask him sometime."

Bradley stares with contempt before turning to exit the terrace. As they walk up the back steps, the detective inquires the meaning behind Tony's comments and Bradley simply responds, "It's nothing."

Dr. Simpson and Detective Dunbar show themselves out of the house.

CHAPTER 18

A TRAGIC ESCAPE

Paige and Bradley go to exit the Reinstad estate. The charcoal sedan waits for the security gate to retract before pulling out into the court. Detective Dunbar however, only drives about twenty feet before she applies the brake and slows the car to a stop.

Not watching the road ahead, Bradley turns toward Paige to acknowledge her hesitance and notices her focus is set straight forward. Bradley finally turns back and looks out through the windshield to see two black SUVs sitting at the far end of lot blocking the exit. Where Sycamore Grove ends and the court entrance begins, a bottleneck point occurs where the SUVs have obstructively parked sideways.

Paige curiously asks, "Oh, what the hell is this?"

Bradley replies, "I don't know, but it doesn't look welcoming."

Four men, wearing black suits, black ties, and black sunglasses, exit the black SUVs (Do all government agents know of only one color?) and stand at attention waiting for Paige's response. The passenger door of the one SUV opens and Dr. Walter Truax steps out.

"Oh boy!" Bradley exclaims.

Detective Dunbar jokes with Bradley, "There's your secret admirer."

Bradley turns and offers Paige a discrepant stare before responding. "I think we've been ratted out."

"I think so too." Paige reforms back into serious mode thanks to Bradley's stink eye and ensuing comment. "You ready for this?" Paige sits up straight and places both hands firmly on the wheel.

Bradley reaches over and grabs the seatbelt and buckles up before responding, "Yeah, let's go."

The detective starts off slowly. The sedan rolls unassumingly toward the blockade while Dr. Truax takes a few steps forward and holds up his hand to halt Paige's approach. By the time Walter walks well into the court, separating himself from his entourage, Paige is rolling steadily towards him.

Detective Dunbar suddenly slams her foot down on the accelerator. The tires spin-out a bit, finally catch, and the sedan rockets toward the unsuspecting Truax.

Walter reacts, "Oh, this crazy bitch is not..." He takes a moment to see if Paige will drive around him but quickly learns that's not going to happen. Walter jumps out of the way of the speeding car and rolls hard on the asphalt of the cul-de-sac.

The government agents all draw their side arms and engage the incoming target. Bullets riddle the sedan.

"Get down! Get down!" Paige yells as she ducks down to avoid being hit while attempting to keep the car on course. Bradley takes her advice, ducks down, and covers his head.

The bullets impact and rip off small pieces of the car. The windshield is shot out, the side view mirrors are shot off, and the grill is being shredded.

Paige aims the car at the left side of the blockade and braces for the impact. The agents fire their last safe shots before they have to jump away from the impending collision. One agent rolls out of the way, resets his stance, and fires a well-timed shot through the broken windshield.

The bullet strikes Detective Dunbar in the left shoulder just as the sedan collides violently into the rear end of the SUV. The truck spins clockwise, causing the front bumper to impact the other vehicle and push it aside. The momentum continues carrying both SUVs until they crash back into one another and are pressed together.

The impact lifts Paige's sedan up on the left side of its chassis. It pushes beyond the obstruction and teeters off the road until a shallow ditch drops the car back down on all four wheels. After colliding into the embankment beyond the ditch, Paige cuts the wheel back towards the road while continuing to floor the accelerator. The sedan's rear-wheel drive spins the tires while kicking up dirt and grasses until it finally adjusts and climbs the vehicle back onto Sycamore Grove and speeds away. The sedan continues to serpentine down the road trying to gain traction over the paved asphalt.

At this time, Bradley looks over at Paige to check her status and sees the blood all over the headrest of the driver's seat. Paige's posture favors her left shoulder making it hard to steer the car. "Oh my god, Paige!" Bradley quickly grabs the wheel and adjusts their direction. He steers the sedan while observing the bullet wound in Paige's shoulder. "Did the bullet exit cleanly?"

Counting on Bradley to drive, Paige takes her right hand from the steering wheel and reaches under her armpit behind her left shoulder. "Yes. I feel an exit wound."

"Keep pressure on it." Bradley suggests.

Paige quickly removes her belt and though the pain is excruciating, she wraps the belt around her shoulder, threads it through the buckle, and pulls it tight.

Bradley leans to his left and against the dashboard, stretching his seatbelt to its limit while trying to steer the vehicle. He tells Paige, "Here, switch me places."

Bradley unbuckles his seatbelt while Paige slides over tenderly until she's under Bradley's body and can remove her feet from the pedals. The car idles for a moment as Bradley climbs over Paige's legs and into the driver's seat.

Meanwhile, Dr. Truax and two other agents climb into the one partially damaged SUV and begin chasing after Paige's sedan. A third agent runs after the truck and eventually works his way to the back passenger door before jumping into the vehicle as well.

The entire rear end and bumper of the other SUV dangles from its frame, and the rear tires have been bent on their axis making them inoperable.

Bradley maintains his speed down the lane though the damage to the front of the car is substantial. He glances in the rearview mirror and notices a black object creeping up behind him. Bradley turns around and observes the threat while informing Paige, "Someone's following us. This isn't over yet." Bradley steps down on the accelerator and pushes the poor, bullet pierced, and smoky engine to its max.

So far, Detective Dunbar is coping with her injury, but Bradley knows she needs immediate medical attention. Unfortunately, he must first evade his pursuers.

Sycamore Grove is not easily navigated. Narrow, winding roads combined with blind curves and a high grade of descent through the foothills will keep Bradley's awareness at a heightened state. He takes to the terrain in an aggressive and unstable manner. The crumpled hood and pushed in bumper rattle further away from secure at every sharp turn, the tires wobble and the alignment is shot, chards of glass from the broken windshield fly backwards through the car and pelt Bradley and Paige in the face, and the black SUV is gaining due to its more powerful and more operational engine, four-wheel drive, and all-weather radials. Other than that, they're getting low on gas too.

Though Dr. Truax hopped in the driver's door, he actually sits in the passenger seat while his good buddy General Taylor drives the SUV. The vehicles careen down the wooded countryside and as the truck approaches the sedan, it shifts over to the left lane and steadies for an attack.

Bradley drifts the sedan left-of-center to cutoff the opportunity for a side swipe. Little time is available to block his shadow from gaining leverage on the road and adjusting the vehicle to make the next turn. The competitive driving bears a strong resemblance to a time trial race for qualification in Le Mans.

Scarce traffic makes it possible for both vehicles to utilize the full extent of the road, though occasional semi trucks and scenic drivers pose a great obstacle.

The SUV knocks at Paige's back fender and causes her sedan to slide and bank on the road. Bradley must work overtime to maintain control after each bump. The energy of inertia applies enough pressure on the car's body that it tends to veer outside and onto the shoulder while rounding each dangerous curve. But thankfully, the galvanized guardrails have since kept Bradley from being run off the road. The vehicle scrapes against the metal barriers causing sparks and pieces of the side panels to fly off in its wake.

Just as before, Bradley does fairly well maintaining the lead over his attackers. The narrowness of the road plays to his advantage and before long the chase begins to reach the end of the foothills. The descent levels out and soon takes a dangerous toll into more residential areas. General Taylor again, attempts to pass Bradley on his left, but a log truck entering onto Sycamore Grove causes the General to quickly brake and swerve back into the right lane. Though empty in its hull, the log truck almost loses control as it squeezes by the battling vehicles. The truck driver depresses his horn and offers a few choice words and gestures to the road raged warriors.

As the vehicles exit the foothills and enter onto a small, residential highway with the city skyline looming in the distance, Dr. Truax gets on his cell phone and updates the anonymous receiver, "We're on Route 18 heading towards the city. He's in Detective Dunbar's sedan. Cut him off." Walter ends one call and consecutively dials another. General Taylor however, swerves in and out of traffic in hot pursuit and the shaking and bobbing troubles Walter's steady hands from making the next call. Walter turns and glares at the General, "Are you having fun over there?"

General Taylor steadies the truck behind Bradley's bumper and keeps pace.

Walter successfully makes his phone call but this time unfortunately, his request is much grimmer, "Execute Detective Dunbar's host program." Click.

General Taylor suddenly accelerates and smacks against the sedan's rear bumper. The impact jolts Walter and his cell phone goes flying out of his hand and crashes at his feet. Walter turns and backhands General Taylor on the shoulder, "God damn it! What's wrong with you? Don't you know how to drive?"

"It wasn't my fault. He braked." General Taylor defends.

"No the hell he didn't. You sped up." Walter reaches down and picks up his cell phone. Thankfully, it's not broken.

Bradley maneuvers through the light traffic quite concise, even with a monkey on his back. He looks over at his wounded cohort to access her condition. Bradley asks, "How're you doing over there?" Paige's face has lost some of its coloring and her weak posture strongly illustrates symptoms of anemia from all the blood loss.

"I'm hanging in there." Paige responds tiredly. She leans back in her chair while holding her shoulder.

Bradley wants to get Detective Dunbar to his office, but he knows he can't allow Truax to follow. Bradley's only option is to try and lose him. He pushes the sedan to almost ninety miles-per-hour. Passing by on the left and right, motorists honk their horns at Bradley's reckless operation, and as the chase nears the inner city, traffic becomes more and more congested limiting Bradley's opportunities to evade the SUV. The sedan's front bumper still dangles from underneath the crumpled hood and continues to scrape against the highway. It's only a matter of time before it breaks free.

After a couple of close calls and minor clips, Bradley notices traffic slowing down ahead and must brake in order to avoid a collision. He quickly tries to change lanes, but a car blocks his exit.

General Taylor takes advantage of the opportunity to catch up and pull alongside the sedan. The General rams the SUV against Paige's car and the collision pushes the sedan right of its lane and into the car beside it, getting pinched. The government agent who initially chased after the SUV to join his compatriots in the fight, lowers his window and takes aim with his sidearm. He fires a three-round burst into the side of the car.

Bradley and Paige duck down as bullets ricochet within the vehicle. Bradley steps down on the accelerator and as other motorists also hear the shots, they react hysterically. They accelerate their vehicles until colliding into the automobiles in front of them. Bradley quickly slams on the brake to allow the SUV and the car on his right to pass. Once free of their clamp, Bradley accelerates into the right lane and then onto the shoulder. He enjoys the available space while General Taylor eventually maneuvers behind him and continues the chase.

The two vehicles speed by the gridlocked traffic, cutting between the cars that attempt to merge from the entrance ramps. Bradley finally notices the exit ramp approaching up ahead and he maneuvers the vehicle toward the uphill route.

The chase enters the city streets. Sirens can be heard in the distance. Bradley just misses being T-boned by cross traffic as he darts through the red light of the intersection, turns right, and heads downtown. The SUV sideswipes the motorist as it pushes through the same intersection to keep pace.

Before long, Bradley and Paige notice something strange. Traffic appears to be dwindling, in fact disappearing to the point where both sides of the street are free and clear. Unimpeded, the vehicles speed down the normally packed city streets. Even the pedestrians stay clear of the road and observe the disturbances as they zoom past.

And that's when Bradley sees it: A police barricade has been setup and it appears an all-points bulletin has been issued as well. Half of the city's police force lines the road ahead.

Paige looks out and comments on the gathering, "It's Captain Garrett's men. Truax must've told him we were coming. You can't let him stop us." Suddenly, Detective Dunbar starts to shake. Her eyes blink wildly while her muscles tighten and begin to spasm. Paige's upper torso begins to seizure and her entire body locks up. "Bradley?" She pleads with a sporadic and trailing voice.

"Holy shit, Paige!" Bradley's frightful reaction causes him to almost lose the wheel. The sedan is nearly at the blocked intersection.

Detective Dunbar mutters another desperate request, "Help me."

Bradley has his hands full now. Between Paige suffering from a stroke, the police blockade dead ahead, and the envoy of psychopaths nipping at his bumper, the stakes couldn't get any higher.

At the last minute, Bradley notices a gap on the left side of the intersection between the light pole and the corner building. He quickly cuts left and squeaks between the obstacles and the multiple cruisers that'd tried blocking the road. A small, coin-operated, newspaper console is positioned near the corner, but Bradley's recalculated route puts the machine directly in his path. The high-speed impact throws the vending machine in the air.

Finally, the collision detaches the front bumper and along with the falling newspaper console, they crash down into the road and leave a field of debris behind the sedan. The trailing SUV runs over Bradley's missing bumper and its front passenger tire suddenly pops. The loss of traction from running over the debris causes the SUV to fail in its turn and at that speed, carry the truck beyond the gap in the sidewalk and directly into the light pole. The vehicle crashes through the pole and into the police barricade beyond.

Officers fire rounds at Paige's fleeing sedan, but they must move quickly in order to avoid the incoming light pole and SUV. The truck rear-ends one of the parked cruisers and pushes it into the neighboring cruiser creating a domino effect. The SUV's front end bounces up and comes to rest on top of the piled wreck while the street light and utility pole finally crashes down on top of the compressed mass of authoritative gaucherie.

Bradley successfully drives away from the close call with very little time to spare.

CHAPTER 19

DEATH OF A DETECTIVE

A busted, charcoal, Ford Crown Victoria, with one white door, no windows, a crumpled front end, and smoke billowing from its engine compartment, noticeably limps into the parking lot of St. John's Medical Center. The bullet riddled, Swiss cheese resembling vehicle sputters to a loud and cloudy stop near the Medical Examiner's entrance.

Bradley jumps out of the driver's door and runs over to the passenger side. Detective Dunbar's condition is extremely deteriorated. Her face is pale white, blood drips from her nostrils and ears, the constant shaking has left her in a cold sweat, and the already existing gunshot wound has drained Paige of all animation.

Bradley rips the car door open and lifts Paige from her blood-soaked chair. He turns and proceeds to carry her through his own personal work entrance. "Hang on, Paige."

Bradley quickly makes his way to the examination room and enters to find Dr. Miller operating on a corpse. Dr. Bryan Miller has done well in Bradley's absence, acting as both County Coroner and St. John's lead Medical Examiner. Dr. Miller turns from his work to acknowledge the visitors.

"Bryan, help me." Bradley asks as he carries Paige over toward an open operating table.

Dr. Miller quickly drops what he's doing and assists in wheeling the table underneath Paige. He holds the table steady while Bradley lays the detective down. "What happened to her?" Dr. Miller asks.

Bradley responds, "She's been shot. But she's also suffering spasmodic episodes. Go get the defibrillator and get it charged."

"What? You can't!" Dr. Miller advises. "It'll stop her heart."

"I know. I know. I don't have a choice." Bradley unbuckles Paige's utility belt as well as removing her necklace and earrings to free her of all metallic material while Dr. Miller wheels the cart that houses the electric shock machine over to the bed. Dr. Miller turns on the machine and it begins charging.

Bradley goes to turn and set Paige's effects down on the table behind him, but Paige grabs a hold of his arm and stops him. She removes her TASER gun from its holster and hands it to Bradley. In a very faint voice, Detective Dunbar says, "Take it. You might need it."

Bradley sets the gun and the belt down on the table before grabbing a pair of surgical scissors and turning back to Paige. Bradley positions the scissors to cut off Paige's shirt. She reaches up and takes Bradley's free hand and squeezes it for comfort. Bradley returns the gesture and assures her, "It's going to be all right."

Detective Dunbar lays back and releases Bradley's hand. Bradley carefully begins cutting her shirt starting from the collar down. Once cut, Bradley spreads the shirt open and places two shock pads on the bare skin of her upper chest and mid-rib area.

An alarm beeps on the defibrillator to indicate operational readiness. Bradley places a rubber guard inside Paige's mouth to protect her teeth from clamping together and possibly shattering, or to protect her from potentially swallowing her tongue.

Bradley quickly grabs the two paddles and positions them over the shock pads.

"Are you sure about this?" Dr. Miller asks as a final intervention.

"Yes." Bradley holds the paddles down on Detective Dunbar's torso and says, "Clear!"

The machine sends it shock into Paige's body causing her back to arc, her jaw to lock up, and her teeth to bite down. Detective

Dunbar's body then goes limp and falls back to the table. Her head slinks to the side while her heartbeat and breathing fails. Detective Paige Dunbar is officially dead.

Bradley turns to Dr. Miller, "Make sure she doesn't show any signs of brain activity or we'll have to hit her again. She needs to be inanimate for at least twelve hours."

Dr. Miller asks, "What are you going to do?"

"I'm going after the ones who did this. In fact that reminds me, she can't stay here. They'll be looking for her. We have to find a place to hide her body." Bradley turns and pockets Paige's TASER gun along with grabbing her utility belt. He takes a medical blanket from the nearby table and covers the detective's body. Dr. Simpson and Dr. Miller both take a side and assist in rolling the examination table out of the room.

Bryan and Bradley proceed down the hallway. "I got an idea." Bradley exclaims after viewing the sign for RADIOLOGY. They wheel the table around the corner and almost collide into Superintendent, Dr. Marco Pascoli as he walks the corridor.

"What's the rush, fellows?" Dr. Pascoli recognizes Bradley guiding the one side of the table. "Dr. Simpson, I thought you still had three days before your leave was up?"

"Detective Dunbar's been shot." Bradley explains. "It was Dr. Truax's men."

Dr. Pascoli quickly interrupts, "First off, Dr. Simpson, do yourself a favor and shut the hell up. Dr. Miller, you may return to your work promptly. I'm sure Dr. Simpson and Detective Dunbar appreciate your help, but I've got it from here. Dr. Simpson, if you would, follow me." Dr. Pascoli turns and starts off down the hallway.

Bradley turns to Dr. Miller and they both share a moment of confusion. Bryan slowly turns and starts back to his examination lab.

"Thanks, Bryan." Bradley puts his hand on Bryan's shoulder before he leaves. Eventually, Bradley turns and follows Dr. Pascoli.

Dr. Pascoli suddenly stops and turns back. "Oh, and gentlemen? Remember, this never happened." While Dr. Pascoli withdraws and continues walking, he urges, "Come, Dr. Simpson," Bradley abandons Paige and begins to follow empty-handed. Dr. Pascoli takes notice and replies, "Bring your patient with you, Doctor. We can't just leave her lying in the hallway." Bradley recollects the hospital bed and pushes Paige in Dr. Pascoli's direction.

The Superintendent leads Bradley through the double doors of the Radiology Department, to the end of the corridor, and left into a series of isolated observation rooms. The radiation warnings offer a good deterrent from anyone searching the premise. Dr. Pascoli picks a small room off to the side and props the door open for Bradley to wheel in Paige's body. Bradley pushes the bed into the center of the room while Dr. Pascoli closes the door behind him.

Marco continues through the room and walks passed Bradley. He speaks to him firmly but with a strange hint of compassion. "I know you like to wear your emotions on the sleeve of your shirt, Dr. Simpson, but your lack of discretion is endangering." Dr. Pascoli engages certain medical monitoring equipment and places sensors on Paige's body to ensure the proper handling of her chances for resurgence. He continues speaking, "Did it not occur to you that there are others who support the Magnus split? Your ability to attract attention to yourself does nothing but put a target on your back. So far, I'd say your investigative process reminds me of nothing but a bull in a china shop. I know it's too much for me to ask that you lay low, but you don't exactly possess a killer instinct either."

Bradley had a feeling that Dr. Pascoli knew what Truax and the other members of the Trust were trying to accomplish, but he doesn't understand the reasons behind Marco's cautiousness. Bradley asks his boss, "What do you know?"

Dr. Pascoli responds a little to Bradley's surprise, "I know that the only way for you to get your life back is to forever change something, or to forever accept something. As much as I didn't want Neurolex in my facility, I'm still alive to do something about it. The question is, Dr. Simpson, is how far *you* are willing to go? How much *you* are willing to risk?"

"I can't turn back now." Bradley takes a step back and looks at Paige. "Take care of her." He turns and starts out the door.

Dr. Pascoli stops him, "Where are you going?"

Bradley turns back and replies, "Philadelphia. I left something back there. By the way, I need to borrow your car."

Dr. Pascoli smiles and says, "The keys are in my office. In the coat pocket. Be careful, Dr. Simpson. And don't worry, I'll clean her wound and start the transfusion."

"Thanks, Marco." Bradley takes a long look at Detective Dunbar.

Marco assures him, "She'll be fine."

Bradley turns and heads for Dr. Pascoli's office.

Dr. Walter Truax and his entourage of three government agents stroll through the main entrance of St. John's Medical Center and march directly toward the Medical Examiner's office. Walter pushes in the door leading to Bradley's personal desk to only find it empty. A following search in the examination room next door turns up similar results, short of one Dr. Miller who swears he hasn't seen Bradley lately. Truax informs his men to spread out and search the hospital room by room.

Bradley turns the corner after exiting the Radiology Department and sees the agents all entering into different rooms while Dr. Truax walks off in the direction of Dr. Pascoli's office. Taking what might be his only chance to sneak past, Bradley quickly walks down the hallway right by the preoccupied agents and around the corner to follow Walter. He keeps at a distance and thankfully, because of all the other people walking the hallway, he doesn't have to creep along the walls, or hide behind drinking fountains, or anything else obstructively covert.

Dr. Truax makes his way through the central lobby and into Dr. Pascoli's office while Bradley walks around to the opposite side of the lobby, beyond the hospital's administrative center, and into the gift shop. Bradley is looking over the selection of plush teddy bears with the words, "Get Well Soon," sewn into their bellies when Walter emerges from Dr. Pascoli's office dissatisfied. Bradley reaches up and grabs a toy bear to avoid eye contact with Truax. Walter scans over the lobby considering his search options before he continues down the hallway toward Emergency Admittance.

Bradley attempts to leave the gift shop but an astute clerk questions him on why he's leaving with one of their teddy bears without paying first. Bradley sets his adorable decoy back on the shelf and continues on with the objective.

For some reason, Bradley decides to tiptoe across the lobby. To the puzzlement of other witnesses, he keeps an eye on Truax's direction until finally reaching Dr. Pascoli's office door. Still in his sneaking fashion, he enters over the threshold and realizes, "Just grab the damn keys." Bradley approaches the overcoat hanging on the wooden rack in the corner and collects the contents from its pocket. Suddenly subservient, he puts the keys in his own pocket and exits Dr. Pascoli's office.

Bradley then makes for the freight elevators whereby Marco parks his car near the corresponding loading docks. Bradley must wait for a janitor and cart to exit the elevator first, but he soon boards the transit heading downwards toward B1.

The elevator doors open up and sure enough, there sits Dr. Pascoli's Victory Red, 2015 Chevy Camaro, with two white stripes running parallel down the center length of the car. Bradley disarms the security system, opens the door, and sits down into the light brown leather interior. He takes a moment to gawk over the lavish design and modern dashboard amenities. Once content, Bradley puts the key into the ignition and fires up the engine. The aggressive roar of the engine offers function and ferocity similar to a lion declaring his dominance over the pride. "Man, that's damn cool!" The good doctor can't help but spin the tires a bit while pulling out of the parking lot.

Bradley must first stop at the house before taking to the road again. As fun as the drive would be in Marco's muscle car, Bradley can't shake his guilt enough to put the miles or drain the gas in his boss's ride.

Bradley pulls onto his street expecting half of the city's police force to be waiting, but to his surprise it's just his truck. He parks next to old reliable and hurries inside the house.

The trip to Philadelphia is nothing more than emergency override. Bradley really has no idea what he's going to do when he gets there.

The empty house offers a quiet overcast that's strangely panic-stricken. Bradley quickly ascends the living room stairs and into the bedroom for fresh supplies. The high impact obstacles that the day has presented beckons a proper shower and a change of clothes, but he doesn't wish to waste so much time as investing in more than a washcloth and a new outfit. However, one particular item does place high on Bradley's list of priorities: Audrey's three-fifty-seven Smith & Wesson six-shot revolver. It might come in handy.

Still brandishing Paige's TASER gun as well, Bradley gathers his essentials and gears up for battle.

Now, the investigative process has taken on a whole different level for Dr. Simpson. His next target: His wife and son.

The low afternoon sun glares but yet graces Dr. Simpson's impulsive decision to play the heroic messenger. Traffic is relatively light though offering its own sporadic upheavals, but the road is long and extremely tedious. Bradley's attention span trails off and his eyes become heavier after each passing mile. A modernized and conveniently well conceived ding warns the weary driver of the vehicle's depleted fuel. Bradley must stop for a refill.

The random exit that Dr. Simpson chooses in accordance to the sign on the highway that bears a symbol assuring there's a gas station nearby, turns out to be quite the charming setting. Or as some might say: A cozy little nook. Not one hundred yards off of the exit ramp, a gas station, diner, and motel crop all-in-one, offers a quiet, comforting appeal that mimics a small village in the Swiss Alps or someplace where random outcrops of cottages and boutiques offer very specialized and traditional design. The one-story, hardwood structures with a Dutch looking architecture, boast strength and durability to the point where Bradley wonders if they weren't just recently built as a tourist attraction, or if they've simply stood the test of time.

As much as Dr. Simpson wishes he could join in the homey congress due to his exhausted state and if he's not mistaken, the second time he's driven this route today, but Bradley knows he must get to his family as quickly as possible.

Because the pumps or even the cash registers lack today's modern digital upgrades, Bradley concludes that this quaint little villa has simply stood the test of time. He walks into the station's entrance and finds it to resemble a hunting lodge more than a convenient store. Between the darker color schemes, the stone chimney and fireplace against the back wall, and the wood trim with beheaded animal décor spanning the surround, Bradley knows he's either in the midst of wilderness luxury or desperate cabin fever. The kind of feeling that gives banjos a bad rep.

Bradley pays cash. Since the clerk doesn't know how much "Fill'er up," costs and the fact that credit cards don't exist out here, Bradley hands him sixty bucks and goes about his way.

Once fully fueled, Bradley continues his unguided venture somewhat disappointed that he didn't stay at the beautiful lodge, but still disconnectedly relieved to get the hell out of there untouched. (Literally.) Though nothing really happened, the place just had this creepy, unsettling, all-in-the-family vibe.

Bradley is a couple of hours outside of Philadelphia when the sun finally fades below the horizon. The dark road is long and boring, but Bradley's adrenaline has driven his tired, baggy eyed, zombie like demeanor to the brink. Upon nearing his in-laws abode once again, he decides to call his wife and warn her of his approach as well as devise a plan. Bradley grabs his cell phone and voice dials Audrey on the speaker.

She answers, "Bradley?"

And as the good doctor often does, "Hey, honey. How's it going?"

Audrey is much too firm to deny her candor. "Where are you? Are you all right?"

Bradley responds, "I'm fine, I'm fine. I was wondering if you could meet me at the wishing well. I have something for you."

"Sure. When?" Audrey asks.

Bradley's designation, "In one hour."

Click. Bradley quickly disconnects the call with his wife.

CHAPTER 20

LAST CHANCE TOGETHER

1:22 AM. Bradley pulls up next to the large pool outside The Philadelphia Museum of Art. It's the usual meeting spot from their past. Audrey and Bradley spent many romantic nights there courting their blossoming relationship. They nicknamed the spot the wishing well because of their longing desire for nuptials. The subtle lighting accents the grandeur of the surrounding scenery even amidst the darkness of night.

Audrey anxiously awaits her husband's arrival supplementing her time with a circumventing pace. But she knows his news must be dire or why else would he travel to such lengths? The passing shine of headlights ignites Audrey's curiosity to the point of willfully enacting her premeditated dubiousness.

Bradley hops out of the door of his SUV and walks toward his wife with a gift in hand. Before he can even offer an explanation for his presence, Audrey opens with her own consideration. "Bradley? What's the matter? What's wrong?"

"Relax. Nothing's wrong." Bradley insists. "I've learned things. I guess I just didn't realize that there were certain consequences to what I started."

Audrey remains concerned, "What is it? What did you learn?"

Bradley hesitates and takes a deep breath before speaking. "I know you never believed me about the bugs, and the whole cover-up, and everything else. But I love you, and I don't want to see anything happen to you. I'm not crazy, Audrey. This shit is for real." Bradley takes another moment and tries to gather his thoughts for proper conveyance. "I learned these bugs can be distributed through contact or as an airborne contagion."

Audrey interrupts, "What does that mean?"

"It means that anyone I've come in contact with is susceptible. You, Jacob, everyone." Bradley can't help but hide his remorse out of duty and decree.

"Oh my god," is Audrey's response.

Bradley urges his gift forward, "Here, take this."

Audrey looks down at the TASER gun in Bradley's hand and somewhat confused, she searches for a peaceful understanding. Without a decisive conclusion, "What's this for?" is the only thing she can come up with.

Bradley breaks the news, "Chances are, you've all been infected. It just depends on to what extent?" He takes a step closer to his wife. "This is for your protection." Bradley hands Audrey the gun. "If anyone starts acting strange, like compulsive or seizure like symptoms, it can be used to overload the circuitry in these machines and kill them."

Audrey asks alarmingly, "You mean I have to electrocute someone to save them?"

"Yes." Dr. Grim replies.

"Bradley, I can't." Audrey confirms. "I can't use this on our son. My parents, not a problem. But not Jacob."

"Audrey," Bradley informs, "It might be the only thing that can save him. Hopefully, we'll never have to use it. I just want to be prepared, that's all."

Bradley takes a step away from his wife and begins to turn back to the SUV.

"Where are you going?" Audrey asks her husband.

"I'm going after Truax." Bradley reveals the true nature behind this sudden excursion. It appears to be more of a last chance to say goodbye rather than a desperate defense relay.

"Bradley, no." Audrey stops the good doctor's departure. "Look at you. You're exhausted. Come back to the house with me."

"No, I can't." Bradley stands firm. "I have to do this. I've come this far, I can't turn back now."

"No, don't give me your lone, gunslinger, hero speech. Listen to yourself. All you said was I. You are not alone in this fight. You keep making this a personal issue." Audrey slowly approaches Bradley as he stands with his back turned.

Bradley can't face her. "They've already tried to kill me three times. And they shot Detective Dunbar. Someone has to stand up to them, or no one will. Like Dr. Pascoli said, you either forever change something or you forever accept something. I will not accept this." Bradley steps away from Audrey as she attempts to put her hand on his shoulder. "I will return."

"Bradley!" Now Audrey must stand firm. "Give me the gun."

Bradley stops and turns back, "I already did."

"No, the other one." Audrey stares at him with an unwavering conviction to ensure his well-being and to quell his rash decision making.

Bradley finally lowers his eyes and reaches into his coat pocket. He pulls Audrey's three-fifty-seven revolver from its hiding place. Bradley shamefully walks over to his wife and hands her the gun.

Audrey instead, takes Bradley's arms in her hands and she holds him tight. "Stay with me," she pleads.

"I can't go back to the house." Bradley exclaims. "I don't want to have to deal with Marge and Roger."

Audrey clarifies, "No. I mean here. Stay *here* with me."

"Where?" Bradley wonders while looking around for suitable lodging.

"I have my father's truck. The back seats fold down." Audrey explains.

Being that Bradley always needs to have the essentials at his side, he asks, "What about blankets or something? What if we get cold?"

With a suggestive grin, Audrey says, "I think we can find a way to stay warm."

"I don't know." Bradley attempts to stay focused on his pre-formed mission but Audrey pushes herself in close.

"I do." She says softly. "We have the whole place to ourselves. And we have all night for each other. Let's take it."

After not *too* long of a deliberation, Bradley surrenders to his wife's proposal. They take each other in their arms and share a kiss before eventually climbing into the back of Roger's Lincoln. (Nocturnal activities abound.)

7:15 AM. The next morning, the two lovebirds are suddenly awoken by a firm knock on the window. A city cop out on his beat happens upon two vacant vehicles illegally parked at the museum.

Audrey and Bradley quickly spring into action from the sound of a Mag-Lite banging against the glass. Audrey lowers the tinted window and asks, "Can I help you, Officer?"

The cop enlightens her, "Ma'am, are you aware that there's a parking limit here of only two hours?"

"Sorry, Officer," Audrey exclaims. "We were just getting ready to leave."

"We?" The cop asks, not yet having seen Audrey's bungalow buddy. He shines in the light to further investigate the disturbance and notices not only her counterpart in the vehicle, but the fact that both of them are scarcely dressed. "Oh, you've got to be kidding me?" He exclaims, having gained full attention. "You two should be ashamed of yourselves. This is a public park. Children play here. You would expose their innocence to this gross sexual misconduct? What the hell's the matter with you? I should have you both run downtown."

Audrey defends her decision while rallying to get dressed. "I'm sorry, Officer. You're right. We'll be gone in no time."

"Make sure you do." The officer warns. "And don't ever let me catch you hippies here again, or I *will* place you under arrest naked or not. Now get dressed and get the hell out of here. And don't touch anyone."

"Yes, sir." Audrey vivaciously rolls up the window with embarrassment while the cop continues walking his beat. She turns back to Bradley and sees the shit-eating grin on his face. "What the hell is so funny?" She asks.

"This was your idea." Bradley lies back down and crosses his arms behind his head enjoying the lighthearted dysfunction of the morning. It sets a gentle focus toward the day's pace.

Once Audrey and Bradley finish clothing themselves, they exit the Lincoln and prime for their departures. The cold chill in the air sparks Bradley to remote start his vehicle while unlocking the doors and adjusting the heat. With the driver's side door ajar, Bradley turns back to his wife and preps his goodbye.

"What do you plan to do?" Audrey asks.

Bradley admits, "Well, I planned on going in there with guns blazing, but that plan fell through."

And in classic Audrey fashion, "No. You see, that's why I took the gun from you. Men always think that violence solves problems, but it just delays them. Why don't you go in there and just tell him to stop or you'll take it public."

"Yeah, see that's when the violence starts. And I'm going to wish I had my gun." Bradley rebounds with a comical accuracy.

"It's not even your gun." Audrey dampens the criticality of the moment. "Trust me, if you go down that path you'll think it's the answer to solving everything. That is something *I* will not accept. You're better than that."

Though the Simpson and Hilliard families hold their argumentative grounds quite well, their unfailing and undying critiques prove beneficial counsel.

Bradley again, accepts his wife's proposal and lowers his head in search of strength and resolution. "In truth, I don't know what I'm going to do. I just know I have to do it."

"Why?" Audrey's question actually stands very pertinent. "What's driving you?"

Dr. Bradley Simpson finally decides to shed a little insight on what sparked his initial determination. "I grew up hearing grim stories about government and corporate corruption. How it holds people back. How the politics keep people from helping each other without settling the bill first. The red tape. I came into work one day and found I was responsible for telling the public, and family members, how six of its most prominent businessmen, or persons, where suddenly gunned down all at once. People should have the right to live their lives in comfort, with a clear conscience. They deserve to have their trust restored through results, not promises. They deserve the truth."

"And you're going to bring it to them?" Audrey questions a possible delusion of grandeur.

Our hero responds, "I'm going to try. Maybe that's where everybody else failed." Bradley takes a step forward and leans in to kiss Audrey. "I love you." They exchange their sign of devotion before Audrey reaches up and rests her hand on Bradley's face.

She tells him, "Be careful. Be patient."

Audrey watches as her husband turns and marches toward his vehicle. She can't help but feel somewhat compelled to assist in Bradley's heroic assault, but the surrealism of the moment creates an apprehension that cements her triumphant spirit to the floor. He climbs into the vehicle and backs out.

While Bradley drives off, Audrey's growing guilt and conflict of interest tells her one thing: A decision has to be made.

Bradley again makes his way back to a displaced and broken home, a shattered reputation, and a suffering career. Even though it's Saturday morning and he's supposed to return to work on Monday. Not to mention those individuals still trying to kill him, the main difference is that up to this point, Bradley has simply followed leads. But now, he must constitute change.

CHAPTER 21

POINT OF NO RETURN

The final quest.

Bradley navigates the open road with ease, only stopping once for gas. Unfortunately, he chooses not to revisit the little backwoods refueling station-slash-cottage that he encountered on the journey into Philadelphia. Bradley enters the outskirts of town just after two o'clock in the afternoon, but before he goes straight for his target, Bradley must first plan his approach. The first stop: the liquor store.

Bradley then takes his journey back home. A feeling of comfort comes over him as the sight of Dr. Pascoli's Camaro still sitting in his driveway reinstalls faith that his absence went unnoticed, at least domestically. He parks the SUV and heads inside the house.

Considering the fact that Bradley hasn't properly showered since the night of his electroshock therapy session, he concludes that a thorough revival is in order. He sets the water as hot as a man can withstand to cleanse contemptible egomaniacal impurities and the coast is set.

Fresh out of the shower, Bradley decides not to dress in mediocrity consisting of polos and khakis or slacks and a fancy button-down, but opting for a three-piece, black-on-emerald dinner suit. It's about as James Bond as he can muster.

Bradley preps for his endeavor accordingly and makes his

exit out the front door. Though he wouldn't mind borrowing the Camaro again, Bradley's pretty sure this final journey will involve a few bumps in the road and subjecting Dr. Pascoli's ride to whatever transpires weighs on his sense of responsibility. So it's the Mercedes SUV with the reconnected rear end.

Bradley heads out of town passing by the newly reopened *The Avenue* restaurant on his way. He'll have to stop in sometime later to see what they've done with the place.

The SUV enters the foothills and begins its ascent. As usual, traffic is nonexistent except for the occasional logging truck or the pickups that the City Engineers Department employs. Bradley finally makes his way to 11405 Sycamore Grove, or as the sign reads: N.E.T.I. Pharmaceuticals. The facility rests only a few miles short of the turn off into Heritage Court.

Bradley pulls up to the gated entrance and alongside the call box. He presses in the call button and waits for a response.

Meanwhile...

Back at St. John's Medical Center, Dr. Marco Pascoli rests comfortably in his desk chair reading the morning paper. Adorned with a large cup of coffee blended with Amaretto creamer, he takes up residence in a small office space that's tucked within the Radiology Department. Only a few feet away, lays the unresponsive Detective Dunbar.

As Marco takes a sip from his mug, a system for monitoring brain activity suddenly beeps. The high chirp mimics a response from a heartbeat monitor, but this chirp engages an electroencephalogram. The needle shuffles up and down on the page a bit and then runs flat.

Dr. Pascoli keeps a sharp eye on the monitor, but soon returns to his paper. Then another beep suddenly sounds. The signal starts off sporadically before it begins to steady.

Marco jumps up from his seat and runs over into the other room. Detective Dunbar's brain activity starts pushing off the charts. The needle on the EEG scribbles wildly across the sheet. Marco places two fingers on the side of Paige's neck but is disappointed when he can't find a pulse.

Suddenly, the needle spikes and goes dead. A violent spasm lifts Detective Dunbar's upper body into the air. Her muscles tense and cause the back to arc high and the mouth and eyes to involuntarily open. Detective Paige Dunbar springs back to life with a violent scream.

Dr. Pascoli shields his ears as Paige quickly sits up wide-eyed and unsure of her surroundings to not only scan over the room, but to try and cope with the nausea and dizziness that follows her splitting headache. It doesn't take the detective long to figure out that she was just shocked back to life quite similar to the manner in which she was dispatched. Paige tries to calm her nerves and focus on the strange figure sitting across from her. She finally concentrates her vision on Dr. Pascoli.

Marco declares, "Welcome back, Detective Dunbar."

Back at N.E.T.I. Pharmaceuticals...

Bradley is finally greeted over the voice box. "Can I help you?"

"Yes." Bradley answers. "I'm here to see Dr. Truax."

The voice responds, "I'm sorry but Dr. Truax isn't available. And this facility does not accept personal visits."

Bradley is able to gather a smirk on his face before replying, "Ah, but I'm his favorite patient. Just let him know I'm here. You'll see, he won't be disappointed."

The other end of the transmission clicks off the receiver and Bradley is left with the hollow scratch of open air. He sits back and waits patiently like his wife prescribed.

Before long, a different voice returns, "Dr. Simpson. I'm so glad you could join us." Assuming from the mechanically distorted voice that it's actually Truax, Bradley opens with an oratorical sense of calm.

"Howdy, Walter. Mind if we shoot the shit for a minute?" Dr. Simpson doesn't intend on approaching the situation lightly.

"Not at all. Please, pull around to the back." Apparently, Walter doesn't play for prose either.

Bradley does as he's instructed and pulls his vehicle alongside the structure and around to the back parking lot. He steps out of the ride looking very dashing and debonair for the task at hand. Bradley reaches back into the truck and makes sure he arms himself with a fifth of Wild Turkey bourbon as well as a small trinket that he swiped from the kitchen drawer, and then heads for the rear entrance. After a quick tip of the bottle and a little rap on the corner of the brick pillar that supports the entrance's overhang to ensure a hairline crack in the glass, Bradley lifts his booze hand and presses the button beside the security door for admittance. He cares not to conceal his weapon while waiting on an insider to buzz him through the door. This is sure to be one of Dr. Simpson's greatest acts.

The buzzer sounds on the steel doors and Bradley pulls open the entrance to his final objective yet first castle. He opens his act with an over exaggerated stagger down the main corridor. Taking small sips from the bottle as he zigzags up and down the hallway, all the while leaving a trail of booze in his wake, Bradley ensures attention is both gained and exonerated through mutual behavioral repugnance.

Before long, Dr. Truax, accompanied by his military entourage consisting of General Taylor and the squirrelly agent who shot Detective Dunbar, turns the corner and approaches Bradley from down the hall. Walter opens with the greeting, "Dr. Simpson, it is certainly inopportune for you to show up here in this condition."

Bradley fires right back, "Well, if it were up to you I'd already be dead. So I'll take my chances." He tips the bottle again and enjoys the crisp, smoky goodness provided by the aged barrel.

"Well, nonetheless," Walter retorts, "This is not the appropriate setting to make a spectacle out of yourself. Please, follow me. We can talk privately."

"Oh that's right, you guys like to keep things low-key. I forgot." Bradley follows his escorts with both his effects and his poise well-in-hand.

Dr. Truax leads him down the same corridor and into the central control hub just outside the decontamination room that attracted and later infected the curiosity of his military guinea pigs. Our hero however, has plans of his own.

Bradley steps into the control room while the door electronically seals behind him.

"Would you care to take a seat?" Walter offers as he circles around to the one side of a small conference table that centers the room.

Bradley responds, "No, thank you. I don't plan on staying long."

Dr. Truax and the squirrelly agent both take a seat while General Taylor and Bradley choose to remain standing. General Taylor crosses his arms and stares at Bradley with contempt while Bradley places one hand in his pant's pocket and maintains a grip on his bottle with the other.

"So what can I do for you, Dr. Simpson?" Walter asks.

"I don't quite know how to say this, Walter. So I'll just say it. You can stop." Bradley responds confidently. "All of this. Stop manufacturing these bugs. Stop subjecting innocent people to your corruption. Stop lying to everyone. And stop sending your G-Men after me all the fucking time. If not, I'll exhaust my every effort in trying to bring the truth to the public and put you son's of bitches out of commission once and for all."

Walter leans back in his chair with a conspicuous smirk on his face before explaining, "I'm sorry, Dr. Simpson, but you're in no position to be making threats. For three reasons: One, we don't manufacture the bugs, or biometric organisms as we like to call them. That takes place at a separate facility. We simply program them. So not matter what you do here, they will continue being built. Two, you can explain to the public all you want about the truth of our plans. We'll see how many of them actually believe you. You'll dig your own grave. And three, we've been administering various applications like this for over three decades now. Don't you think that if there was a way to expose and bring down the system, it would've already happened? You're just wasting your time. You've always been wasting your time."

Bradley offers no pardon, "Well Dr. Truax, that's exactly why I'm here. I came because I wanted to start making a difference. I came to change something." Suddenly, Bradley slams the whiskey bottle against the top of the conference table and shatters the glass.

Whiskey, along with chards of glass, splash up and impact not only General Taylor and the other agent, but Dr. Truax as well. The majority of the contents pour off the table top and saturate the squirrelly agent sitting to Walter's left, but some slightly douses Truax in the process. Both men stand from their chairs and begin swiping the alcohol from their clothes.

General Taylor actually reaches for his sidearm when Bradley takes the offensive, but the sudden burning from whiskey in his eyes causes him to reprioritize.

General Taylor rubs at his eyes while Dr. Truax speaks out against Bradley's behavior, "That was cute." Walter attempts to brush the excess bourbon from his jacket and also his face. He squints in an attempt to cope with the pain. "Now what exactly was *that* supposed to accomplish?" Walter asks as he tries to regain focus.

Bradley responds, "It's to start a fire." He finally removes the one hand from his pant's pocket to reveal the match that he'd been quietly concealing. Bradley took the match from the kitchen drawer where they're only kept for the purpose of lighting birthday candles or the grill on occasion, but that's only if the electronic igniter craps out. Bradley strikes the match on the heel of his shoe and ignites the sulfur capsule into a small, orange, football shaped object of potentially massive destruction.

This time, General Taylor aims his sidearm with conviction and steadies his sights.

"No, wait!" Walter pleads with Bradley.

Bradley stands firm and offers a simple response, "This is for Phil, you son of a bitch." He throws the match on top of the alcohol-soaked conference table and it bursts into flames. The fire instantly spreads.

General Taylor takes his shot, but since he doesn't calculate the time it takes for the fire to jump from the table to his jacket, his defense mechanism causes his arms to raise and the bullet to miss high. The fire catches on his sleeves and parts of his chest. He tries smacking at the fire with his sidearm while attempting to unzip his jacket.

The squirrelly agent doesn't fair that well. One drop of enflamed alcohol falls from the table and ignites the saturated floor. The fire works quickly, engulfing the agent's shoes before moving up his legs to the middle body or lap, and eventually to the stomach and upper body. The agent screams in agony.

Bradley can't help but yell out, "That's for Detective Dunbar, you piece of shit!" Bradley also has to jump back and away from the flames. The soles of his shoes have actually caught fire from stepping in the alcohol and he decides to stamp his feet wildly in an attempt to asphyxiate the hotness, sort of resembling a bad jig.

Dr Truax receives a similar threat to that of the now enflamed agent. The fire ignites his shoes and pants. He bats at his legs and knees trying to halt the flames advance, but that just ignites his hands and sleeves. Walter leaps away from the enflamed table and runs from the fire. He runs over to the control panel and activates an emergency contingency that releases the electromagnetic pulse after a three minute delay.

By now, the fire alarm system has also recognized the threat, but the sprinklers are delayed by Walter's faulty program override. Since the central control system can't come in contact with water, the reprogrammed function offers the computer system a delay to properly shut down while allowing emergency evacuation procedures to be implemented before releasing any water. Unfortunately, that's when all hell breaks lose.

The override automatically unlocks and unseals all the electronic doors. Before, the system used to lock down every room for containment and specimen preservation purposes, but an accident twelve years ago demonstrated that those still inside could not always be evacuated in time, thus becoming trapped and either burned alive or killed from smoke inhalation.

Bradley watches as the control room doors open and the fire races outward into the hallway. During the conversation between Bradley and Dr. Truax, various employees, technicians, and lab workers passed nonchalantly throughout the facility to perform their duties unaware of the trail of bourbon they were spreading. The fire follows their footprints and veins off from the central corridor into corresponding labs while simultaneously, peculiar isolated incidents occur elsewhere.

While lab workers prepped for the clean rooms, they put on a type of neoprene shoe cover to avoid contamination. Unfortunately, while sliding the covers over their soles, their surgical gloves accidentally contacted the alcohol which later causes spontaneous combustions from the constant shocks they apply to stimulate their specimens for diagnostic evaluation. Lab technician's hands start catching on fire in various parts of the facility.

Now Bradley truly has started a fire. All that's left for him to do is escape.

The sprinkler systems finally activate and douse the control room. A partially burnt Dr. Truax and General Taylor flail their arms and tap their chests to extinguish the flames. Parts of the main control panel spark and pop from the water, but the prior shutdown should've preserved memory and certain software data.

The sprinkler systems work fast to catch up to the fire but that simply adds to the damage. All the specimens throughout eighty-six percent of the facility are fried from active operating equipment short-circuiting and electrifying the now flooded containment dishes. Certain high security labs are not affected by the emergency system being they support their own independent utility and lockdown procedures, but the pulse will soon discharge.

While the General and Dr. Truax were putting out their own fires, Bradley took the opportunity to make a break for the control room doors. General Taylor responds first and fires a shot at the fleeing escapist of administrative ascendancy, but his bullet catches the frame of the door and Bradley's able to successfully exit and head down the corridor. General Taylor quickly makes chase after Dr. Simpson while Walter slowly follows behind.

Walter however, having suffered more serious wounds than the General, doesn't follow the chase down the corridor. He turns right after exiting the control room and heads toward the building's front entrance to try and cutoff Bradley's getaway.

General Taylor stays roughly thirty feet behind Bradley in the crowded hallway of evacuees. There are just too many people in the way for General Taylor to get a clear shot, recklessly enough though, that doesn't stop him.

Bradley glances over his shoulder in time to see General Taylor take aim. Bradley ducks to the side and covers his head.

General Taylor squeezes the trigger and the bullet strikes a fleeing lab worker in the back.

Bradley decides to yell out, "Gun! Everybody down!" The request proves to accomplish the same as an ambulance's siren. Everybody moves to the sides of the aisle and then ducks down to the floor. The sudden move offers Bradley a clear path to the exit, but regrettably, it also offers General Taylor a clear shot on his target. Bradley continues toward the exit while the General steadies his aim and fires.

The bullet strikes Bradley in the lower left shoulder and exits cleanly just under the clavicle. The force of the impact pushes Bradley forward and into the wall of the narrow entryway. He spins off of the wall leaving a bloodstain on the point of contact, continues his momentum, and exits through the facility doors out into the parking lot.

General Taylor pursues his target, but a surprise group of systems monitors following the evacuation rush out from a side corridor and directly in front of the General's path. He accidentally runs into the back of one of the operators thus slowly his pace and giving Bradley the head start that he needs. The General frantically pushes through the cloud of nerds in a hopeless determination to fulfill his duty.

Bradley wastes no time in reaching his SUV or pressing the button on the key fob to unlock the doors and maintain pace to escape alive. He hops in the truck and fires up the engine.

General Taylor successfully navigates the speed bump of geeks and pushes through the back doors in time to see Bradley peel out and head for the front gate. General Taylor opens fire on the truck till he empties the clip, but Bradley safely drives off. The General continues running after the vehicle.

Employees are flooding the exits and pushing out into the parking lot when the electromagnetic pulse is released. The blue light races through the facility, beyond the exits, and reaches a small portion of the surrounding area. Dozens of infected workers who're still inside or in close proximity of the facility, suddenly drop like flies. The burst of magnetism violently shocks the recipient's brain and they simply shut down and expire.

Bradley is halfway down the drive when the digital display in his truck fails from the blast. Fortunately, the engine stays true. Unfortunately, he doesn't even notice. He instead, notices the strange figure standing in front of the exit gate. As he approaches, Bradley recognizes Dr. Truax acts as the last line of defense. Bradley is now faced with a conundrum: Does he just run Walter over, end all of this, then make for his getaway and have the guilt of murder following him around at every turn? Or should he spare Walter, avoid the gate, and attempt to drive through the electrified fence? There's no time for a split decision.

Bradley chooses to steer the vehicle away from Walter and spare himself the guilt of lowering to their level. Bradley punches the accelerator and braces for whatever happens. The SUV slams against the fence and the barrier buckles outwards. The barbed wire and electric cables stretch to the point of snapping, but the fence itself won't give way. Electricity charges the truck before the fence's connection is severed and fries it's every relay switch leaving the SUV dead in its tracks. The vehicle scrapes to a stop alongside the fence and becomes trapped in the mangled weave of metal.

Bradley has to climb out through the rear hatch and actually jump from the vehicle in order to avoid grounding himself to the electrified frame. He rolls in the grass before standing up to see both Walter and General Taylor have closed on his position. General Taylor has his sidearm reloaded, aimed, and ready to fire.

Walter offers the comment, "You've come to the end of the line, Dr. Simpson."

Bradley's slumped posture favors his left side. He's lost a good amount of blood from the gunshot wound in his shoulder. Bradley stands beaten and out of options to make a last desperate attempt for survival. Maybe Walter's right and he's come to the end of his fight for truth and justice.

Walter makes one final comment as Bradley accepts his defeat, "I'm sorry, Dr. Simpson. You had a good run, but your involvement with this corporation is over."

General Taylor steadies his gun and aims at Bradley's center mass. Bradley opens his arms wide and closes his eyes in fearful anticipation.

Suddenly, the loud screeching of a vehicle's tires catches everyone's attention. Bradley opens his eyes to see a silver 2015 Lincoln Navigator veer off the road at full speed and crash through the security gate. Audrey decided to commandeer Roger's ride once more.

She keeps the pedal to the metal and steers the vehicle right at General Taylor. General Taylor stands his ground and opens fire on the Lincoln, but Audrey ducks down and avoids the bullets as they impact the windshield. She stays on course and slams the truck dead into General Taylor sending him and the gun flying through the air. General Taylor's lifeless body bounces off the ground and rolls to a stop while the gun falls to the grass closest to Walter.

Audrey quickly hits the brakes and jumps out of the vehicle. Walter runs over to the General's gun and picks it up off the grass.

Walter aims the gun at Audrey.

"No!" Bradley cries out.

Audrey however, surprises both of them when she quick draws her three-fifty-seven revolver and fires a shot dead into Walter's chest.

Walter is able to get his shot off, but the force of Audrey's bullet pushes his upper body backwards and his aim goes high. Walter staggers for a moment and looks down to observe the wound in his chest before he finally falls to the ground. Dr. Walter Truax, member of the Medical Board of Trust and Chairman and CEO of N.E.T.I. Pharmaceuticals is dead.

Bradley can't help but display his awareness, "I told you, you better hope she doesn't have a pistol."

CHAPTER 22

SMOKE OVER THE SKYLINE

The oddly calm Audrey turns and makes her way over to her wounded husband with a hero's stride still grasping the gun in her hand as she walks. Our original hero has been saved for now.

The sound of multiple sirens fades into range as the authorities near.

As Audrey approaches Bradley, he slowly sinks to his knees. Audrey quickly runs over and kneels down beside her husband before asking him, "Bradley? Are you all right?"

"I think I'll make it." He responds. "I've lost a lot of blood." Bradley's pale frame sways unsteadily from the anemia.

Audrey tears at the hem of her T-shirt until she rips the entire ring from the bottom. With a cut from her pocket knife, the hem is reutilized into a temporary tourniquet. She wraps the cloth around Bradley's shoulder and ties it down tight. Bradley somewhat winces from the pain, but he won't cry out.

The fire trucks arrive first, followed by the fire marshal's personal vehicle. Then shortly after, the boys in blue consisting of five cruisers and finally the ambulances. Though the sprinkler systems controlled the fire, smoke continues to billow from the vents in the facility's roof.

Evacuees start to appear down the drive from the rear parking lot. Groups of firemen make their way over to the displaced lab workers while two of them approach Audrey and Bradley. One of the firemen asks of the stranded, "Are you two all right?"

"No." Audrey responds. "He's been shot."

The fireman offers closure, "Relax, ma'am. Paramedics are on their way."

The police officers spread out and inspect the situation as two bodies lay in the front yard of the compound. Both Dr. Truax's and General Taylor's identities are recognized immediately upon recovery. Meanwhile, an unmarked cruiser pulls up and adds to the congestion. Captain Garrett exits his vehicle and instructs his men, "Arrest that man."

To Audrey and Bradley's surprise, Captain Garrett is pointing at them. And Bradley is pretty sure that Audrey isn't the man in which he's referring. The firemen stand aside as the officers begin to gather around Bradley's and Audrey's vulnerable sanctuary.

Captain Garrett is also closing in on their position when another set of sirens suddenly fades into recognition. This time however, the sirens belong to an ambulance and the police chief's cruiser. The vehicles pull in behind everybody else and screech to a halt. Chief Martin Alvarez and Inspector Dempsey step out of the vehicle to engage the status of this event while an unexpected duo hops out of the ambulance.

"No! Let them go!" An unknown voice declares.

Captain Garrett along with his fellow officers as well as Bradley and Audrey, turn to see Detective Dunbar accompanied by Dr. Pascoli and wielding a state of defense for the fallen liberators.

The undead Paige Dunbar marches hence forth to clarify the authority's inaccuracies. She walks up to the Captain and informs him, "The Chief would like to speak with you." Captain Garrett is forced to leave the assembly.

Dr. Pascoli comes jogging along with a duffle bag full of first aid gear.

"Stand aside." Audrey commands of the officers. She walks

through their defense circle and leans over to check on Bradley. "How're you holding up?"

"Top notch." Bradley responds.

Detective Dunbar shares a smile with Audrey before she stands up to allow Dr. Pascoli room to work.

Marco grabs a roll of gauze and a bottle of rubbing alcohol so that he can begin cleaning and dressing Bradley's wound. He instructs Bradley, "We need to get you to the hospital for a blood transfusion."

Bradley ensures him, "I'll be all right. How about something for the pain?"

Dr. Pascoli smiles as he takes a syringe full of morphine from his duffle bag, removes the plastic cap off of the needle, and firmly stabs Bradley in the leg.

Bradley jumps back in pain. "Ouch! What the hell was *that* for?"

Dr. Pascoli responds, "For the fun of it." He finishes dressing the wound before asking, "How does your shoulder feel?"

"It feels fine. It's my leg that hurts like a bitch now." Bradley doesn't take too kindly to Marco's form of therapy.

"Good. Then I did my job." Dr. Pascoli stands and though Bradley seems a little puzzled by the treatment, time allows both Bradley and the morphine a chance to settle. After a moment, Marco asks, "How do you feel now?"

Since it takes Bradley a second to decide which injury hurts worse, he automatically assumes that the morphine is taking effect. Audrey, somewhat comforted, finally stands from her husband's side and joins Paige and Marco in the observation.

Dr. Pascoli leans down and offers Bradley a hand, "Are you ready to go?"

Bradley answers, "No, not yet. Just let me sit here for a couple of minutes."

Dr. Pascoli, Detective Dunbar, and Audrey all give Bradley some space. They turn and survey the crowded scene of flashing police cars and fire trucks, authority figures trying to get things under control, large water hoses that have been drug from their corresponding trucks and into the facility, and smoke still rising from the once formidable N.E.T.I. Pharmaceuticals compound. A few employees lay in the front grass as firemen and additional paramedics tend to their smoke inhalation. Cops gather and question anyone in sight to not only gain clues on the fire's origin, but to explain the mass of bodies scattered throughout the facility and piled up near the rear entrance. The remaining paramedics carry two covered bodies on stretchers from the front yard and to the open doors of nearby ambulances.

Dr. Bradley Simpson sits in the grass of the foothills overlooking the city skyline that looms in the distance. Smoke has gathered well enough to distort his visual clarity, but the underlying threat still lingers. His body is bruised, battered, and bloody. After being stabbed, shot, electrocuted, and in multiple collisions, three separate bandages cover his left shoulder, his chest, and his left bicep. As he sits there pondering over his perilous journey thus far and events yet to come, Bradley can't help but wonder how many other broken men have gazed upon this ominous skyline and longed for absolution? He knows this fight has only just begun, and against a very formidable opponent. The public will expect answers for what transpired here today, but after that, the attack on capital must commence.

Bradley takes one last glimpse upon the structured wilderness before he readies to leave. He's sure that Dr Pascoli probably wants his Camaro back by now but unfortunately, Bradley needs a ride to the hospital first. He only has one day left anyways before he has to return to work on Monday. Bradley already knows what Dr. Pascoli will ask of him, "How was your vacation?" (Struggle never subsides.)

The true folly of man is a system of belief where ignorance offers bliss and that what you don't know can't hurt you. Good luck.

ABOUT THE AUTHOR

Remi Albert is a Warren, Ohio, native and a graduate of Warren G. Harding High School, studying theater and writing at Ohio University. He works part time at a local hardware store in his hometown and writes in his spare time.